ANYTHING FOR HIM

LILY HARLEM AND NATALIE DAE

mischief

Mischief
An imprint of HarperCollins*Publishers*
77–85 Fulham Palace Road,
Hammersmith, London W6 8JB

www.mischiefbooks.com

A Paperback Original 2013

First published in Great Britain in ebook format by
HarperCollins*Publishers* 2012

Copyright © Lily Harlem and Natalie Dae 2013

Lily Harlem and Natalie Dae asserts the moral right to
be identified as the author of this work

A catalogue record for this book is
available from the British Library

ISBN-13: 9780007553310

Find out more about HarperCollins and the environment at
www.harpercollins.co.uk/green

CONTENTS

Contents

Chapter One

I stared at the photograph he'd emailed me. He'd promised he would and, finally, it had arrived.

It wasn't what I'd expected; not that I thought for a minute he'd send me a copy of his passport photo; but this, this had really taken me by surprise. The odd angle of the camera lens and the overwhelming suggestiveness shocked me. It was deeply personal, completely voyeuristic and undoubtedly the most erotic image I had ever laid eyes on.

But it gave nothing away of the face I longed to see; yet, it told me so much about the man I'd been obsessing about for weeks. I reached over and clicked the printer to life. As it clanked through the setting-up motions, I leaned closer to my computer screen and allowed him to fill my vision.

His long, pale, black-hair-coated shin was in the forefront of the picture. The knee flopped wantonly towards the camera, making the patella the largest thing in the frame. His foot was out of shot. Beyond his leg, I could make out the right side of his torso – just – a small amount of lean waist, a hint at a taut set of ribs and a balled shoulder leading to what looked like a busy hand. I say busy, because he appeared to be jerking off, but of course, that could just be my filthy imagination.

His head was thrown back, his chin jutted upwards, his prominent Adam's apple in profile against the bottle-green wall behind him. Other than his chin, not one facial feature could be identified, but what I saw of his chin, chiselled and dented at the centre, led me to believe the rest of his face would be angular and long.

Seedy shadows doused the whole image, the covers on the bed dusky green, almost brown, and the lighting, maybe shining through a cheap drawn curtain, was dim.

He seemed completely uninhibited despite the camera, which I guessed was on a timer. I gulped down a bite of bile as a sudden wave of regret at the photo I'd sent him rolled through me. I'd thought I was being sassy, original, beating him at his own game. But it was clear now that I played with someone who knew how to think out of the box, stay a step ahead, out-manoeuvre me without even needing to try.

The printer creaked to readiness and I hit the print button. I had to have his image in my hands, laser scanned, details ripe for scrutiny. As it whirred and heaved and slowly spat out the paper, I paced my office-cum-artist studio, frantically scratching the tops of my arms with my nails.

Damn that picture of my right areola. Not that it was a bad areola or a bad picture, it wasn't. I was perfectly pert and the pixel count excellent. I had even rubbed an ice cube around my tight nub, before pulling it to a painful point, then, as a final creative flair, shined a spotlight on it. The dark room and bright light had made my wet skin golden, my nipple a rosy pink. The round-tipped point was blood-filled, the flesh leading to it wrinkled in an ordered, twisted way, as it strained to seek out more stimulation.

Damn that picture. His wasn't exactly classy, but it was artistic, unique, risqué. Mine was just a token rude shot, though at least I'd resisted a shot of my newly shaved pussy. I would be in cringing hell right now if I'd followed through with that plan.

The next question was, of course, would we meet? We'd had a deal – if we liked the look of one another we would make arrangements for a date, a face-to-face encounter. Although, judging by the dirty routes our conversations had taken lately, I reckoned there would be considerably more than just our faces meeting. At least that was what I hoped.

So, my answer to 'should we meet' was a happy-dancing 'yes', my panties wet just from the sight of that bony shin and jauntily jutted head. The image of him alone, masturbating, thinking of me, possibly, had me so turned on my clit bobbed and my nipples were as tight as when they'd been treated to that ice cube.

But what about him? Would he think me unimaginative, boring, dull? The trouble was with Liuz, he was so articulate, so self-assured, and despite his first language being Polish, his mastery of English was excellent. Not that mine isn't too. I'm a journalist, studied at Canterbury, and I'm also an artist, but somehow he always seemed to second guess what I was saying, or going to say, in my emails.

I held the newly printed-out photo in the air, the paper warm on my fingertips. I enjoyed having it A4 size, and peered closely.

I could make out the dark shafts of his leg hairs winding out of his skin, the creases on the sheet below his body wrinkled like ripples in water. Perhaps, also, I could make out a burn of black-fuzzed hair coming down in front of his ear, but I couldn't be sure. It could be more of the stubble that coated his neck.

After retrieving a couple of drawing pins from a purple, sparkly pot on my desk, I hung Liuz's image on my pin board, right in front of my desk. Where I could gorge on it; for when I looked at him, a fraction of the need, the burning want inside me, was sated.

Taking a deep breath, I did what I had to do next – check my in-box. We're in the same time zone now that

I'm back from my business trip to the United States, so he could have possibly seen it already. Plus, as a general rule he was at his computer. I wasn't sure exactly what he did, but he worked from home. Marketing he'd said, something about buying and selling stock.

In-box. One new message.

From him.

I sucked in a breath and opened it. Those few seconds it took to process were absolute agony.

'Your picture arrived.'

A rippling tightness in my guts had my belly tensing. Did he like it? Did he think I'd cheated by sending him so little to go on when he'd offered up so much? Given me such an honest picture that showed him vulnerable, a label I never would have given Liuz.

Quickly, I typed a response. Typical me, I avoided the pressing point. 'So did yours.'

'And what did you think?'

'I think you look like you are enjoying yourself.'

'Mmm, enjoying or just taking care of an urge? A necessary task, if you like.'

'So which was it?'

'Which would you rather it was?'

I hesitated for a moment, then decided to risk a knock-back. 'I hope you were enjoying yourself. I hope you were thinking of me, imagining you were fucking me.' I hit send and waited for a response.

Nothing.

One minute stretched into two.

I stood and flung open the window to the autumn morning. Immediately, sounds of the city filtered up. Car horns, bus engines, the shouts of the workmen several buildings down.

Another message. About bloody time.

'I was thinking of you, but not about fucking you.'

'What then?'

'Ah, that's for me to know and you to find out, Aniolku.'

I clicked my tongue against the roof of my mouth in frustration. He often did this, refused to answer something or turned it around on me. Also, if he knew he was playing coy, or being shifty, he'd nearly always add on 'Aniolku' at the end. I'd asked him what it meant a few weeks ago. He'd told me it was 'angel' in Polish. I'd laughed and said that surely by now he knew I was no angel. His reply was that was what made it such a perfect endearment for me.

'Is that your bedroom?' I asked, desperate to know more about the picture, and in turn, learn more about Liuz.

'No, it's my mate's bedsit.'

'Really?'

'Yeah, really.'

'Did he take the picture?'

'LOL, no, I was alone there. He just happens to have a nice camera.'

'Wouldn't he mind you spunking out on his sheets?'

'I'm a big boy, I can control where I come. I've also heard of tissues.'

A rise of heat flushed over my chest, and I squirmed on the seat. Just the image of long, pearly jets of cum, spurting out onto that lean torso and dribbling into dark body hair, turned me on ridiculously. I could only imagine how his groans of pleasure would sound, how ragged his breaths would become, and what his sex-sweat would smell like, taste like.

I wanted to know all of these things for real. I wanted to know every tiny morsel of information about Liuz more than anything else I'd ever wanted to know.

There was an extended pause, then he typed, 'Yours didn't reveal much.'

'I thought the idea was not to give too much away.'

'You mean you were playing a game with me, and here was I thinking that we were just swapping honest photos of one another.'

'Yours is hardly a mantelpiece portrait.'

'Depends what else is on the mantelpiece.'

An image of his home came to my mind, created entirely in my imagination. He'd told me nothing other than that he lived in a mate's bedsit in Brixton. Sharing or not, I wasn't sure. But now, after seeing the photograph of his friend's place, I visualised something painted in muted colours; moss green and muddy-puddle brown. Sparsely furnished with daylight penetrating curtains, bare bulbs. I don't know why, but this image thrilled me so much more than the thought of a living space neat and ordered, pristine and thought-out. Liuz spent his time immersed in his work, head in his computer – well, either his work or indulging in teasing, flirting and sometimes downright rude talk with me – so I imagined his place would be functional rather than decorative.

'OK, I should have given you more to go on,' I typed back.

'No worries, you have a nice tit. I can tell it would be a good handful and your nipple is perfectly suckable.'

I read that last line twice, and my areolas tingled deliciously at the thought of his mouth on me. Blood rushed to my entire breast, and my nipples pressed into my thin cotton bra. I circled my right nipple, the one on the photograph, over my clothes and allowed the stiffening sensation to bloom.

'Would you like that?' he replied before I could respond to his last email.

'Yes.'

'What else would you like, Aniolku?'

'What else would you do?'

'You mean after I curled my tongue around your nipples, stroked my hands over your breasts and fed

8

you deep into my mouth, pulling you in, devouring you, making you moan for more?'

'Yes, what else would you do?'

I had my hand inside my bra now, plucking and pulling at my nipple. I wished it was his hot mouth, hard and urgent, not gentle – rough and demanding was what I wanted, what I yearned for.

'What would you want me to do?' he asked.

Damn him always throwing questions back at me. I closed my eyes. I had to write something. I knew him well enough by now to know he wouldn't respond until I did.

Once again an image flooded my mind. It was a lewd, sordid image of me, on my knees. A threadbare carpet beneath me and a bare light bulb above. I was naked, naked and submissive. Before me stood Liuz, tall, lean, golden-skinned, holding his cock towards my face. A beautiful cock, fat and generous in length, the glans engorged and the cleft below the head deep. I could see a drop of pre-cum nestled in the slit, and I could hear him telling me, 'Lick it off, whore. Lick me, suck me. Do as I say.'

These images were new to me, sinfully wicked, and generated a well of guilt at what they suggested I really wanted, deep in my soul. But I couldn't ignore them. Something about Liuz and the way he was with me had drawn rank thoughts and lusty needs to the surface; allowed them out to play, if only in my mind. It seemed they had moved in, for a while at least, and I couldn't ignore them.

I settled my fingertips over the keyboard and nibbled on my bottom lip as I wondered what to write. Nothing too crude, but something a little edgy. Eventually I settled on, 'Next I want you to pretend my mouth is your hand. Do what you did to yourself in the picture.'

'You mean jerk into you hard and fast. I don't wank like a delicate little flower, you know.'

'I can imagine.'

'I'd back you up against a wall and hold your head tight. Forge in and out without a thought for your breathing. After all, my hand doesn't need to breathe, does it?'

My heart raced. 'What else?'

'I wouldn't give a shit about whether or not your gag reflex was killing you. I'd ram down your throat, enjoying the wet tightness. And I'd shout at you too.'

My fingers shook as I typed. 'What would you shout?'

Lust screeched around my system.

'That you had to suck harder, open wider, then when I was about to come I would shout at you to swallow, to keep swallowing until I told you to stop. I would keep ramming into you until my bollocks were drained and my cock started to soften.'

I stroked my clit through the gusset of my leggings and gave in to a few deep rotations. I knew I would have to masturbate soon. The need was building, a carnal pressure that would soon require release. One-handedly I replied, 'OK.'

There was long pause, which allowed me to fret myself to an ass-clenching state of arousal; then he answered, 'We should definitely meet.'

I'd sneaked my devilish fingers into my panties now, and the glossy pea that was my clitoris took a hard and fast beating. Once again, I typed 'OK' then, as I hit send, I arched my back, reared my hips off the seat and allowed a sharp climax to take control. I panted through the waves of pleasure. I squeezed my eyes shut and once again visualised Liuz before me, thrusting his dick into my mouth, over and over and over.

Our meeting couldn't come soon enough.

Chapter Two

Four days later Liuz hadn't sent any emails with a fixed meeting date. I found myself getting anxious. I wanted – no, *needed* – to meet him sooner rather than later. My lust for him was growing by the second, and any further delay would likely send me into a tailspin.

On a day when I had absolutely nothing planned, my mind as equally idle as my computer, I wondered why Liuz hadn't contacted me at all that morning. I usually had correspondence from him to wake up to every day, and this was the first time my in-box only displayed spam for penis enlargement and breast augmentation. It got me to thinking about cocks and tits, then Liuz and me. By mid-afternoon a thought came to mind – a totally irrational and insane thought.

I would go to Brixton.

Such was my obsession with him that, as I dressed, I dallied with the idea that fate had made us meet; therefore, fate would direct me to his neighbourhood and we would know one another as soon as we made eye contact. I knew it wasn't normal behaviour, to indulge in such fancies and even believe they could possibly be true, but that was obsession for you. It drove a person to entertain the ludicrous, to imagine the impossible.

I called in a couple of favours from fellow journalists with connections who could do a quick check on names and addresses. I'd wondered if his name was really Liuz; after all, he could have made that up for the purposes of using the internet anonymously, but somehow I didn't think he had. He'd always been honest, blunt a lot of the time, and him being so self-assured made me think he'd be comfortable enough to use his real name. Without a surname to go on, though, the results of the check might have been fruitless, but hey, I'd got lucky. And don't forget, fate was my friend.

Armed with my notebook containing three possible addresses of men named Liuz in Brixton, picked out of the database using God knew what search words – and I didn't want to know – I boarded a bus. Seated next to the window, with my bag on the chair beside me to prevent anyone sitting there, I gazed out at the passing scenery – houses, the odd open space here and there with scant trees, people out and about – seeing them as a blur, focusing my mind on other things.

Like Liuz's picture. Our email conversations. The way he made me come with his dirty words.

I imagined he'd be so pleased to see me when we finally did meet face to face. But what if he wasn't? Yes, I was intrepid online – wasn't everyone, hiding behind a façade of brimming self-confidence and ultra-awareness of how alluring they were to the recipient of their emails? Now, I allowed myself to wallow in insecurity and doubts, nearly biting one of my long, beautifully manicured nails in the process before I stopped myself. I wouldn't want him seeing me with ugly hands. Along with my tongue, pussy, ass and mouth, they were the tools I'd use to seduce him.

I dug into my bag and brought out my compact mirror, flipping it open to take a good look at myself and see what someone saw when they met me for the first time. I wasn't bad-looking, but I wasn't exactly drop-dead gorgeous either. But then, hadn't Liuz been able to come with just my words, sight unseen?

It would be OK, I was sure of it.

And then another thought arrived, fresh from its swift entrance into my mind, all blustery and full of importance.

What if I don't fancy him?

I'd imagined him to be so sexy, so handsome, that I hadn't entertained the idea he might not be to my tastes visually. His words had been enough, hot and lurid, straight to the damn point, but would they be enough once I'd set eyes on him for real? I wasn't a fool; I knew appearances mattered. I'm not shallow, honestly I'm not, but a girl's got to find *something* about the outer package in order to have a connection.

I huffed out a breath and slipped the compact back into my bag, terrorising myself about him not living up to my expectations and me not living up to his. I succumbed, putting one fingernail in my mouth and lightly running the tip across my teeth, then snatching it away, chewing the inside of my cheek instead. What if it all went wrong? Would it be better to just keep it as an online thing?

I tried to envisage never meeting him, never having his hands on my skin, his breaths tickling the back of my neck, his cock inside me. I couldn't do it. I *had* to meet him and, like we'd said, if we didn't like the look of one another then there wouldn't even *be* a meeting – not one that went anywhere anyway.

It'll be all right. Honestly, it'll be fine.

The bus lurched to a stop, the movement shunting me forward, and I flung my hand up to grab the back rail of the seat in front. A middle-aged man got off, stepping down onto a residential street strewn with litter that had undoubtedly been jostled by the wind from an untied refuse sack. As he walked off up the road, a white paper napkin chased him, winding around his ankles like a starving cat unwilling to be ignored. He stopped walking, bent down to catch a hold of it, then balled it into a meaty fist. As the bus started up again, I stared across the bus and out the opposite windows at him, wishing he'd see me so I could gauge his reaction to my looks.

Since when had I become so in need of assurance?

Since I knew damn well this wasn't a game any more. Since I realised he was serious in wanting to meet.

I was serious too, but deep inside, even though I'd gone along with it, even though I'd told myself we'd be meeting, I hadn't *quite* believed it. Easy to be swept along, just like those pieces of litter, and easy to convince myself I could do this thing. And here I was, taking the initiative, a step outside what we'd agreed. Why? Because I wanted to gain the advantage, of seeing him before he saw me. Perhaps, if I did manage to catch a glimpse of him today, and liked what I saw, it would give me the courage to go home and press for a real meet. The problem was, Liuz tended to call the shots. Even though I played the game too, gave the right answers, behaved as though I had all the confidence in the world, it was clear he was the more dominant one.

But wasn't that what I liked so much about him?

Absolutely, and the idea of him being so dominant in person, in bed, had me squirming in my seat. My face flushed at the images flickering through my mind, of our sex-sweat bodies, hands slippery from that and my juices, his cum. Of my hair, lank and damp from exertion, held tight in his steel fist. Of his lips, barely touching my earlobe, filthy words spilling from his mouth in a torrent. Filthy enough to make me come without him touching me.

The bus bell, loud and abrasive, jerked me from my reverie, and I looked about, feeling foolish for having indulged in fantasies when I was supposed to be watching out for the first of my stops. Relieved to see I hadn't missed it, I paid attention to the streets outside, swallowing to combat the sudden dryness in my throat. Another stop and it would be time for me to get off.

That stop came all too quickly, but conversely, not soon enough. I was a tangle of emotions, the threads of them writhing inside me to form several knots that rested hard and dull in my stomach. I wanted to spy on him and I didn't. I wanted to spot him and I didn't. I wanted – God, I wanted far too much. He'd made it that way too, with his dirty emails that set me on fire and gave me a taste for needing more out of sex than a quick fuck that always left me feeling like something was missing. As though what had happened hadn't quite been enough. I wanted more than five minutes of fumbling foreplay, a few sloppy kisses and a cock only sliding in and out enough times so the man could come. I wanted to be lavished with attention, used in ways I'd only ever dreamed about – and left so spent I couldn't walk without my legs almost giving way.

Liuz would give that to me. He'd told me he would. He'd promised.

17

A church spire in the near distance caught my attention, its bricks ancient, that dirty grey only old buildings can wear and still look good. Clouds hung around the stone cross on top, their bellies almost black, distended with rain that would pelt down sometime soon. I quickly checked in my bag, cursing myself for not bringing an umbrella. With no time to chastise myself any longer, I reached up to press the bell then gripped the blue metal pole until the bus stopped once again.

I stepped onto the pavement, its surface ravaged by cracked tarmac, and thanked my lucky stars I hadn't opted to wear heels. I couldn't cope with them on a day like today, where I'd possibly be doing a lot of walking and standing around. With the knots in my belly tightening, I made for the church.

The first address was quite close to it, and I arrived in short time. I stared at the house, one that didn't fit my image of Liuz at all. It was clearly owned by someone well-to-do, all mullioned windows and a nicely tended front garden that spoke of the owner having fingers even greener than the short-clipped lawn and the animal-shaped bushes. He couldn't live here, could he? He'd mentioned a bedsit not a home like this. Unless he'd been lying?

Taking a deep breath, I pushed open the white-painted gate and walked up the short gravel path to a front door that came straight out of a magazine I'd written an article for entitled *Perfect Homes*. It was a double effort, the glass panels diamond-leaded and coloured in transparent hues of red, blue and green. I reached the three steps in front of it and went up, nerves thrumming, my mind screaming that I could do this, that I could pull it off. I was a journalist, for God's sake! I couldn't begin to count the times I'd knocked on someone's door in the hope they'd give me the information I sought.

But I hadn't wanted to fuck those people. I hadn't said rude things to them, exposed my disgusting desires. Exposed my nipple in a picture.

Biting my lower lip, I raised my hand and, before I could talk myself out of it, pressed the brass bell button. The chimes rang out inside, a melody only the rich could get away with without coming across as crass; the echo of each note indicating the house either didn't hold much furniture or it stretched back quite a way, bigger than it appeared from outside.

A blur of movement behind the glass from the far reaches, and then a figure appeared, a slim female if I wasn't mistaken.

Shit. What if he's married?

The door swung open on silent hinges, and I saw I *had* been mistaken. A slight male, maybe mid-twenties, stood on the threshold, hair immaculate in a swept-back style that oozed hair gel and the obvious half hour it must have taken to achieve that look. His nose bordered on being too thin, and I quickly gave him the once over, noting he wore shorts that showed off a knobbly knee that was nothing like the one in Liuz's picture.

'Yes?' he said, tilting his head.

'Liuz?'

'Yes?' He frowned, his expression that of someone wondering how the hell I knew his name – puzzled confusion, lips slightly parted, tongue darting out just that little bit to wet the seam of his lips.

I hadn't thought this through properly and had no idea what to say next. My mouth worked, no words of explanation as to why I was there emerging.

A surname. I needed a surname.

I eyed the brass doorbell. 'Liuz Brass?'

'Uh, no. I think you have the wrong person.' He pursed his lips, cocking one hip to rest it against the door edge, his frown deepening.

'Oh, I'm terribly sorry!'

Before he could ask me what I wanted with Liuz Brass and how I'd come to be at his house, I dashed down the steps and path, the gravel crunching obscenely loudly. The gate closed behind me with all the finality of a don't-return-here-anytime-soon snap, and I ran down the street towards the bus stop. I only allowed myself to breathe once I got there, plonking my ass down on the seat beneath the rain shelter.

What the hell was I thinking?

I didn't know. What I did know was that obsession drove me, obsession was my master, and that I'd get on the bus when it arrived and continue to my next stop. Although that first encounter had been a mountain-sized cockup, it could only get better from here on out. Right?

The bus came, and I perched on the seat nearest the door, determined to keep my attention on the road and not what lay ahead. I told myself off for losing my cool, for forgetting my journalism training. I was supposed to be fearless, able to work under pressure, and get any and all information needed for a story.

I needed to pretend I was just doing my job. Call on the next Liuz but don't knock on the bloody door this time. Just observe.

Back on the street, I walked on uneven flagstones, the colour indiscriminate and without a name, glancing in my notebook to check the number I needed to find. 78 Woodstone Road. Stuffing the book back in my bag and casting a wary glance at the sky, I kept going until I came to a residence that perfectly matched my thoughts of where Liuz would live. Victorian, four stories, the dusty windows of the first floor visible through a black, high, rusty iron-railed fence with a matching gate. I peered at the front door, pleased to note a grey metal casement surrounding several buttons. This was obviously a set of apartments or bedsits.

Bracing myself for a bit of sleuthing, I walked through

the gate and up the short path to the plain wooden door, painted sunflower yellow, streaked with swathes of dirt and a muddy footprint. I studied the name-tags beside each button. A couple of full names were there, but the rest were first-name initials with the surname. And only one initial was an 'L'. The surname was Biros. Possibly Polish?

A quick movement inside to my right, behind one of two windows, snagged my attention. Bushes grew in a row beneath, stout, unruly branches decorated with an abundance of leaves. I looked at the small patch of grass in front of them, then at the bushes, trying to work out whether they would take my weight without me falling. The windows were too high for me to see through otherwise.

I moved in front of the bushes and gave a silent prayer. Before I could talk myself out of it, I scrabbled on top of them, my footing stable, if a little buoyant. I reached up and gripped the stone windowsill, pushing up to press my nose to the lowest part of the pane. A man sat at the back of a long living-cum-bedroom, at a desk boasting stacks of paperwork, a keyboard, and a large monitor that emitted the glow of a website I couldn't make out. He hunched over, studying the screen, a lock of dark hair flopping forward to cover the eye closest to me. His jeans rode low at the rear, giving me a glimpse of a rather delectable ass-top, and his naked back tapered from a trim waist, expanding to broad shoulders, his muscles prominent and well-toned.

Was that my Liuz?

He reared back in his seat, lifting his arms to lace his hands behind his head, and swung his chair around so he faced me, eyes closed. I caught my breath as I scanned his sharply angled face, long and unshaven, his mouth soft and wide. I studied his chest, a scribble of black hairs at its centre. Straight hair covered his armpits, their direction every which way, and I found myself breathing deeply as though I could capture the scent of maleness just from my imagination alone.

And then, to my horror, he opened his eyes. After a brief flash of surprise he stared at me with a look of indignation that burned my cheeks with the shame of being caught spying.

I started, letting out an insipid yelp, and gambolled about trying to get off the bush. It had other ideas, the branches seeming to sprout hands that gripped my ankles and wouldn't let go. To top it off, the heavens opened, a torrent that fell without mercy, uncaring that it peppered my hair with fat, bullet-like drips.

'Fuck!' I scrabbled some more – and fell backwards onto the grass. 'Oh hell!'

Panicked, I managed to stand on unsteady legs and make it to the short path. A few more steps would see me down the road, out of sight, catastrophe averted. I wanted to be at home so badly I could taste it. I should never have come out.

Rain pelted down harder, bouncing off the path, and an ominous grouse of thunder warned of a bad storm in my future. I reached for the gate, getting the hell out of there my only concern. A creak sounded above the patter of the rain, and I couldn't resist looking back. The man I'd spied on stood in the doorway, arms bowed at his sides as though he thought me a thug that needed a good pasting. Still staring over my shoulder, I fumbled with the now-slippery gate, adrenaline surging through me.

He glared at me. They were the blackest eyes I'd ever seen.

I almost whimpered.

He moved to step outside, and I wrenched the gate back.

He bunched his fists, and I made it safely out onto the path.

Breaths gusted from me, and my pulse quickened, the sound of its thrum meshing with that of the slapping rain. I looked at him again as I prepared to run, but something made me remain in place.

He frowned and brought one hand up to the smattering of dark stubble on his chin, and the brief thought that if this was my Liuz, he'd do very nicely, thank you very much.

'Who the fuck are you?' he asked. 'And what do you want?'

Chapter Three

His voice came as a shock, deep and husky and inflected with an accent I didn't recognise, lilting and rapid, almost sing-song. And the way he said 'fuck' was quick and joined to the words after it, as if they were one.

But something about his voice and aggressive tone injected me with flight instinct. I had to get out of there. This was not how it was meant to be between us. Fate hadn't planned this kind of confused, dishevelled meeting. I had to erase it, now, quickly, before it became irreversible.

Clutching my bag, I turned and covered the side of my face with my palm. How could I let him see me for even another second? My mascara was no doubt running down my cheeks – I could imagine its black dribbles streaking over my wet, burning flesh. My clothes were wet and scrappy. My battle with the shrubbery had left its scars – a small rip in the knee of my jeans and several leafy twigs poked from my socks and sneakers.

I picked up a rapid pace, slapped one foot in front of the other on the pavement, not daring to look backwards for fear of doing even more damage to our destiny. But with each step something told me that I'd just met my Liuz. I couldn't deny what I knew in my heart. Not only his accent, which could be Polish, but also the layout of his bedsit was exactly as I'd imagined. Masculine, sexy, and so damn alluring in a sleazy, impersonal, functional way.

After pounding around the corner, past a paper shop, a hairdresser and a tanning parlour, I finally slowed. His long, toned body screamed athletic. He would be swift, energised. If he truly had wanted me, he would have caught me.

A double-decker bus came with merciful promptness. I stamped up the steps, hurled myself onto the empty backseat and slunk low. Shutting my eyes, I cursed the drips of rain snaking down my neck and soaking through my jeans. Behind my lids, the image of him masturbating came to mind. I swallowed a glut of realisation. The darkly stubbled jawline I'd just seen was in keeping with his picture, as were his long limbs. The wall behind the bed in his room was a dirty, murky green, the bedcovers a nondescript mud-brown. That was where he'd been when he had clutched his cock, worked his shaft, spunked out his cum. He hadn't been at a friend's bedsit at all. He'd been at home, on that bed. The bed I had just seen with my own two eyes.

Why had he lied? Did he rent it from his friend, was that it? Or was he ashamed at the state of the place so didn't want to admit it was his?

I dropped my head into my hands and sucked in a breath. Torment twisted within me. Everything I thought I knew about Liuz was up in the air yet at the same time it was all exactly as it seemed. Exactly as I'd hoped.

His face, dark, brooding, dominant, was the mirror image of the one I'd dreamed of night after lonely night. His body, controlled, honed, was the stuff of my horniest fantasies. Both fear and delight seared through me, jumbling one lust-infused thought to the next then winding it with the knowledge that I'd been dealing with a man so gloriously beautiful, so innately masculine that he surely wouldn't be interested in me.

How could I have entertained the fact that I wouldn't be attracted to him?

The bus jostled to a stop and I stared out the window, gathering my bearings. Lights glowed from houses and lampposts as evening spread over London earlier than expected because of the rainstorm. I was getting nearer to home, moving further from him. Another ten minutes and I would be back in the safety of my apartment, away from the dismally orchestrated meeting with the man I wanted to fuck me more than I wanted to take my next breath.

* * *

My pillar-box red sweater was made of the finest cashmere, an indulgence born from a lucrative story in January, and as I pulled it down over my bare breasts the fluffed material tickled my nipples and smoothed over my flat belly like a soft cloud. I scraped back my hair and snapped it into a bobble, hitched up the base of my favourite sweats and sank my shower-hot toes into woolen socks. I had long since mastered the art of booting up my computer and checking for my emails as I went about mundane tasks such as dressing and drinking.

Sipping a glass of Merlot, I checked for a message from Liuz.

Nothing.

I set down the wine and reached for my pale-blue artist's coat. It was thin cotton and dotted with every shade of acrylic paint imaginable. After shrugging into it, I squeezed out several generous blobs of paint onto my board. I had to commit the images swimming around my head to canvas. The compulsion to do so gnawed at me. If I didn't I wouldn't be able to eat, rest or work.

I stared at my blank canvas collection and nibbled on my bottom lip. Nothing seemed big enough. My desire was to have Liuz as large and as real in the room as possible.

I glanced around.

With a flourish of decisiveness, I tugged off a poster I'd bought recently in New York of the Empire State

Building. Ripped at a signed picture I'd had for many years of Paul Weller playing his guitar.

A tall, thin unit, bursting with books, stood to the left, by the door. I heaved, tugged and shifted it to the centre of the room, finally freeing up a large, plain cream wall.

The perfect canvas.

I reached for a dense brush and daubed it in dark-brown paint. Lifted up high and splodged an outline of Liuz's head. Just the barest shape, no detail – that would be added later.

I carefully angled the brush to create the sharp line of his jaw and the dent in his chin, leaving a space where I would come back to his ears. My heart raced and sweat popped between my breasts. For the second time that day, anticipation reeled within me. Soon I would have him before me, in my room.

His neck was next; not too thick, not too thin. I loaded up more paint and with steely determination squared out his shoulders, my breaths rapid. I was hot, the jumper no longer comfortable with all my twitching, stretching movements.

Frustrated by the necessary interruption, I dropped my brush and pulled shut my curtains. Peeled off my artist's coat and dragged my expensive sweater over my head. Tossed it into a corner. Next came my pants and underwear, and finally my socks. Not bothering to put on my paint-speckled coat again, I lunged for my brush.

Naked and free, I set about painting a chest that rose outwards from the sternum, showing off broad pecs. A neatly tapered waist, lean and stretched. When I reached my favourite place of all on a man's body I paused, rubbed a paint-stained hand across my hipbone and sucked in a breath. Even from a distance and through rain I could tell Liuz had adorable oblique muscles.

As I slowly committed the perfect shape to the wall, I stroked my tongue over my upper lip. The delectable angle between bricked abs and the start of his groin had to be just right to make my picture the masterpiece I wanted it to be.

What would that part of his flesh taste like on the tip of my tongue?

My brush was an extension of my mind, my memory and my lust. High on creativity and spurred on by the image unravelling, I added a low-slung waistband. I'd seen him wearing worn jeans – he'd looked dishevelled but at the same time comfortable in his own skin. An intoxicating mix of self-assured sexuality.

Again I paused.

Stepped back.

I shook my head, tutted, and tried to ignore the dampness between my legs as my plan formed.

Bypassing the first part of clothing I'd begun to draw, I continued downwards, flared the outline slightly at his hips and sketched out muscular thighs. The jeans were no longer part of my image. I wanted him as naked as me.

When I reached the knees I concentrated higher again, adding in the smooth balls of his shoulders and powerful arms hanging at his sides. I was completely lost in my task. My mobile rang and I ignored it. A siren screamed on the road below and I took no notice. My limbs felt free, and my skin buzzed as my swift movements caused air to breeze over it. All that existed was myself and the image of Liuz I was creating. An image that surpassed the photo I had hanging in the room, because it included his face – because soon it would include his cock.

His face was my next stage. With a smaller brush I created a proud nose and eyes that held a lazy, devil-may-care look, the visible lids a fraction big, the brows craggy. His mouth was a severe slash, a bit like when he had shouted at me. It was how I wanted it. I didn't want Liuz smiling. I wanted him stern, commanding. A force to be reckoned with.

I squelched out more paint, not caring about the amount I was using. It was worth it. My stomach growled with hunger and I set about sketching his flopping tendrils of hair. My strokes were thick and heavy, the black paint shiny and textured. Carefully, holding my breath, I swirled a strand over his right eye so that it hung in front as I'd seen it do in his room.

Stepping backwards, I surveyed the effect.

Perfect.

I added the hint of an ear. My laptop tinkled to tell me mail had arrived.

Instantly, I was distracted from my fake Liuz to what could possibly be the real thing. Balancing my brush by the paints, I wiped a caked blob of black from my index finger onto my stomach and brought my screen to life.

I was not disappointed.

'Are you there, <u>Aniolku</u>?'

I whipped my messy fingers over the keyboard. 'Sure, been in all day. Waiting for you to say hi.'

That should cover my tail.

There was a several-minute pause. I sipped nervously on my wine and shoved Simply Red into the CD player. Mick's dulcet tones filled my study.

'You said you were going out to cover a premiere in Leicester Square.'

'I was, but I got involved in a project about Uganda's fair trade imports and lost track of time.'

'Do you do that often?'

'What?'

'Lose track of time?'

'Yes, when I'm working.'

And when I'm painting full-size naked men on my wall.

'And you have been working all day?'

A tingle ran up my spine at the undercurrent of the question. Did he suspect? 'Yes, busy, busy, busy, got to pay the bills. What about you? Have you had any sexy thoughts about me?' I reached for my wine.

'I did, sort of. I was looking at a website about female ejaculation and wondering if you were a spurter when a weird thing happened. This woman appeared at my window, staring in at me, even though it was starting to rain.'

Wine burned the back of my throat. I inhaled but no air went in. With my fist I thumped my chest and eventually dislodged the offending dribble of Merlot. I spluttered and coughed, wheezed and gasped. Finally, breath returned and I re-read his last words.

A woman appeared at my window.

There was no doubt about it. Not now. Today Liuz and I had met. Breathed the same air, walked the same path, connected our eyes in a glorious moment of two fates colliding. But it had all happened so fast and I hadn't been the woman I wanted to be.

I sat my bare ass on the chair and willed sane thoughts. I had to play it cool. There was no way in hell I was going to let him know that had been me studying him as the rain began to pour, balancing in a very unladylike way on his shrubbery and looking through his window like some crazy Peeping Tom.

'That's odd,' I replied. 'Did you know her?'

'No, I had never seen her before. But she looked at me as though she recognised my face.'

'That is strange. Then what happened?'

'She ran off, towards the High Street.'

'Didn't you chase her? Find out what she wanted?'

Thank goodness he hadn't.

'No, I was only half dressed, couldn't be bothered.'

'Why were you only half dressed? Been jerking off again?'

Change the subject.

'No, not today. I was just hot, must have been the humidity before the storm. I might jerk off later, though, thinking of you, thinking of fucking you, from behind, my hands in your hair, pulling your head up to the ceiling so that your spine feels like it will snap under the force of my thrusts.'

'Sounds like a plan.' My pussy clenched at the image of my back bowed by the severity of his tight grip on me. I loved it when he put images into words like that.

'I can imagine how your pussy would feel on my cock, but what about your hair, how would that feel in my hands, Aniolku?'

Ah, I knew what he was doing. I wasn't a journalist for nothing. Probing questions were my business. 'Why?'

'I need to know so I can build up the picture in my head.'

I pulled at my long blonde ponytail. A stab of regret tugged my heart. It would have to go. It was exactly the same as the woman who'd looked through his window this afternoon. 'It's black, and barely enough to sink your hands into. It's short and spiky.' As I spoke I reached for a pair of scissors from my pen pot. Letting my hair loose, I gulped the rest of my wine then began to cut.

'I love black hair,' he responded. 'Short black hair I can grab and pull by the roots. I want to hold your head firm, your ass firmer as I fuck you.'

Shivering with desire, I glanced at my feet. They were splattered with dark paint and each slice of the scissor blades delivered a new creamy tendril to the floor around them. As I watched, several thick strands landed over my toes. On the rise of my left foot, an exceptionally long piece fell and balanced.

'Would you like me to fuck your pussy from behind?' he asked.

'Yes.'

'Why?'

'I think you would do it good.'

'It's more than that.'

'It is?'

'Yeah, I know you by now, Hannah. You're a slut, a dirty bitch. You would like me fucking you from behind because then it's impersonal. I could be anyone taking you hard and fast, using your body to get my release and satisfy my big, fat dick.'

OK, that was it, the time had come. I'd had enough of skirting around the main event. I knew what Liuz looked like and I was more attracted to him than I could have ever dared hope. If we didn't move this on soon I would combust. One-handedly I typed back. 'Why don't I come over tomorrow and be your slut?'

'I never thought you'd ask, Aniolku. I'm getting so bored of my own hand.'

He thought I would never ask!

All the damn time I'd been waiting for him to pose the question and all I'd had to do was ask.

'So whereabouts do you live in Brixton?' I dropped the scissors on the desk and ran my fingers through my short hair. It was about two inches all over, including the fringe.

''78 Woodstone Road, flat 2.'

'What time?'

'Nine.'

'OK.'

'One more thing.'

'?'

'I will leave something on the door handle. You will wear it the entire time you are with me.'

'?'

'Trust me, Aniolku, I know what you need more than anyone else you have ever been with.'

I waited another minute to see if he elaborated on this detail. He didn't, so I went back to painting. My mind whirred as my brush flew over the wall, adding in symmetrical abs and long, hairy shins.

Finally.

Finally we had a meeting set up. At his bedsit too. I could hardly believe it.

I glanced at my watch. It was early evening. This time tomorrow I'd be getting ready to take the bus to Brixton once more. With a sudden flourish, I reached over and displayed Liuz's jerking-off photo on my screen. Hit print, ten copies.

Soon, within hours, I would hear him coming, feel him tremble as his cock spurted into me. There was no doubt in my mind we would fuck tomorrow. Too much had passed between us for it not to get carnal and dirty on our first meeting. Sexual tension sizzled through cyber-space with each email we'd sent, right from the word go. He'd coaxed out my secret thoughts about sex. I'd felt safe somehow, telling him sordid fantasies anonymously. His reactions were always positive, encouraging. When I worried I was kinky he'd replied: 'Aniolku, it is only kinky the first time you do it.'

So now, after all my soul-baring, Liuz knew I had a seedy desire to be taken roughly. Degrading, dirty sex was my thing. He knew full well that a dinner date and movie was not necessary for him to get a fuck. Just a series of perverse, crude emails and an address would get me wet and slippery and spreading my legs.

I was a slut.

I was a wet, slippery slut right now.

As I moved between paint and wall, my thighs smoothed against one another. My clit swelled, peeking from its hood as I started work on Liuz's balls. My breaths were short and gasping, and I was bombarded with images of us fucking in every position. Noisy, sweaty, animalistic.

Within minutes I'd created soft sacs, heavier at the base and the skin loose and hair-coated. I could almost feel them, cool, slightly prickly, a perfect cupped palmful.

Briefly, I paused to look at the photos whirring from the printer. Somewhere in the recesses of my mind I hoped it would give me a clue as to what his cock would be like. Would he have a generous length but a slim girth, or a fat, wide dick and a mushroomed head?

Sloshing more wine into my glass and gulping fast, I had a sudden inspiration; it would be like the rest of him, perfect.

Starting above the testicles, I created a thick, upwards-pointing shaft, then, a fraction before I reached his navel, I fashioned a capped head. Something told me he would be circumcised and this was how I painted him.

With a smaller brush I added in shading, bulging veins and a rim beneath the glans. The slit was central and wide, and I placed a blob of perfect snow white in the middle to look like a pearly drip of pre-cum.

Done.

I squeezed and strummed at my nipples as I admired

my full-size mural. Liuz stood before me, brooding, naked and hot enough to sear my skin.

Grabbing the pile of photos from my printer tray, I then spread them on the floor around myself, covering my cut hair and the new splatters of paint with the photos' cool surfaces. There was only one thing on my mind – an orgasm.

I had to climax, now.

After knocking back the last of my wine, I delved into the desk drawer and pulled out my favourite long black vibrator. I never used to keep it in there, but since talking to Liuz on email, it had made its way into the room I now masturbated in with the most frequency.

Dropping to the floor, flat on my back, I stretched my legs wide. Propped the soles of my feet on the wall either side of Liuz's painted knees. Stared at his cock and delighted in the sliding photographic paper beneath my back and hips. I was surrounded by him. Above me, beneath me. All I needed now was to imagine that greedy, determined cock pumping into me.

I spent only a brief second spreading my natural lube around the satiny plastic head of my vibrator; then I shoved it in, hard and fast, just how he would do it. I arched my back and cried out, and I did not take my eyes from Liuz's cock.

Jerking my hips and ramming the vibrator upwards, I imagined him taking me over and over. I could almost hear the hard panting breaths he would groan out as he forged in, not stopping until he'd penetrated me to the hilt. I snarled through the pain, even though it was my own doing. I didn't want comfortable fucking. I wanted to be ravaged by lust, consumed by desire. I wanted it to be as basic and primitive as it was possible to be.

I clicked a button at the base of the shaft and allowed the vibrating plastic ears to embrace my clit. The action was a signal for my body to seek out release. Within seconds I was climbing, climbing high and rapidly. I wanted to shut my eyelids, and my body was ready to fold in on itself. But I wouldn't let it. I had to come with the image of Liuz before me.

I did. In an explosive burst of contractions and spasms, I allowed my orgasm to rake through my core. I stared at his painted cock, wishing it was in me for real. Pounding, thrusting, jettisoning hot, viscous cum into my pussy.

All too quickly the vibrator had served its purpose and I tossed it aside. But I kept my feet planted on the wall; my pussy, swollen and sopping, opened wide before Liuz for his sulky, unblinking gaze to feast on.

Chapter Four

'Oh my dear God!' squealed Hector, my long-standing hairdresser at Portobello Cuts. 'Darling, what the fucking hell have you done?'

I shrugged. 'I'd had some wine, fancied a change.'

'Bloody Nora, why didn't you call me, anytime day or night, no need for such drastic action when Hec is only a phone call away.'

'From Hell to Hec,' I said with a grin. 'Do your best to tidy it up, and dye it black while you're at it.'

'Black!'

'Yep, black.'

Hector frowned and tutted, his whole body twitching up towards his ears. 'My beautiful Hannah, I only hope this is because you are on some super undercover journalist mission and not that you have gone completely insane. Your lovely blonde tresses have been an advert for my work for many years.'

I sat in the chair and allowed him to drape a shiny

silver gown over my front. 'Absolutely, a top-secret jour-nalist mission that will hopefully be very lucrative and very satisfying.'

He shook his head and ran his fingers through my tufts. 'Black, really?'

'As black as you can make it.'

* * *

Walking along the street I'd previously pounded in pouring rain, I allowed the evening air to swirl around my newly exposed nape. It was a Thursday and people were still milling about, some in suits having worked late or going straight for drinks, and some in casual evening-out gear. Men in nice shirts, ladies in dresses with subtle make-up and jewellery; decent girls who looked as if they enjoyed being wined and dined.

Not like me.

I just wanted to be fucked.

I made my way down Woodstone Road creating a show of searching for number 78 just in case he was watching from his window. My aim was to look like I'd never been to this part of Brixton before. I was a newbie, a blow-in.

My heels clacked on wonky pavers and I brushed down the wrinkles in my short red skirt as I approached. I'd worn the opposite to yesterday. No sneakers and jeans for me tonight. I was no longer the inquisitive woman who'd hung in his shrubbery, splashed down the street and ran for the bus. Tonight I was a slut, a harlot, a woman who was ready to be used for a man's most basic satisfaction.

I opened the gate and climbed the steps to the front door, noticing that his curtains were drawn. They were unlined and a weak light shone through them onto the bushes beneath the window. With a trembling hand, for nerves along with lust had overtaken my body, I pressed the intercom buzzer next to 'L Biros'.

He didn't speak, just released the lock to let me in.

The short corridor, leading to a steep set of stairs, was empty of furniture and people, the walls a grimy beige, and as the front door shut behind me with a resounding clunk, silence enveloped me.

His room, number 2, was the first on the right. I took a deep breath and stepped up to it. Draped over the handle was a piece of purple material, about the length and width of a tie. I picked it up, wondering what it was. Painted on the underside were two big eyes. They were almost comical, bright blue and with long lashes, the whites completely exposed.

I now knew what he wanted me to wear.

A blindfold.

I should have guessed. All day I'd fantasised about what he'd leave for me. Crotchless panties, nipple clamps, a leather collar, perhaps. But none of that was really Liuz's style. He wanted to play a game where he was the one in control with me at his mercy. He was going to do that by taking away one of my senses. Luckily, the game, and the blindfold, suited me very well.

Quickly, I tied the material around the back of my head, allowing a slit between my cheeks so if I strained my eyes down I could look at my feet. I was pleased I'd already seen Liuz. If I hadn't and I didn't know how ludicrously attracted to him I was, I wasn't sure if I'd be able to go through with being fucked by him.

I knocked on the door, the noise loud in the quiet stillness, and willed my heart to slow. My hard nipples abraded the cups of my bra with each rapid breath I took. My pussy leaked, the gusset of my thong completely sopping. Getting carnal and sweaty couldn't come quick enough.

The door opened and I was aware of the heavy scent of tobacco before my wrists were caught by big, strong hands.

'Not tight enough.' The same accent-heavy voice I'd heard yesterday.

'Liuz?'

'Who else were you expecting, *Aniolku*?'

I was tugged into the room and my bag fell to the floor. The door slammed shut and I was pressed up against it. Liuz's hands were at the back of my head.

Fiddling, tightening, compressing the blindfold further and taking away the sliver of light I had. Now it was so taut I couldn't open my eyelids behind it.

I reached forward and touched bare flesh; warm, rippled with muscles and coarse hairs. A quick exploration revealed tight flat nipples and the rise of collarbones.

'You showed me so little in your picture when I gave you so much,' he said, his hot breath washing over my cheek. 'So now it is my turn to look at you. All of you.'

I spread my hands over his shoulders. They were high above me, wide and rounded slightly forwards as his hands explored my nape and my neck, the dip of my throat.

'But we must agree on one thing,' he said. 'Because we are no longer just sharing emails, now we are together for real and I want to give you everything you hoped for. Everything you told me you desire.'

His lips whispered over mine and I parted my mouth, sucked in the muggy air, hoping for a kiss.

It didn't come.

'Kilimanjaro,' he murmured.

I swallowed tightly and slid my hands down over his biceps. They were bunched and solid, huge balls of power waiting to be released. A tremble ran up my spine. He felt so damn big and so damn strong.

'Say it,' he said, cupping my jaw in both of his hands and tilting my head upwards. 'Say "Kilimanjaro".'

'Kilimanjaro.'

What was he on about?

'That's the stop word,' he said, rubbing his thumb over my bottom lip, roughly, and I knew he would be spreading my carefully applied ruby lipstick towards my cheek. 'If something happens either of us doesn't want to happen, we just say "Kilimanjaro" and everything stops.'

'Everything?'

'Yes, absolutely everything. It's not a safe word, Hannah, it's a stop word. If you say "Kilimanjaro" it will stop what we are doing in every sense. There will be no more. The same goes if I say it to you. No more. We are fulfilling fantasies here, and if we are not making the dreams come true then what is the point?'

'What do you mean "no more"?'

'No more communication, no more us. Full stop, end of. Out of each other's lives, forever.'

I couldn't imagine needing to use a stop word – if anything I wanted a start word. I wanted him to get down to the serious business of sating the lust he'd been building within me over these last few weeks. 'OK. Stop word. Kilimanjaro.'

He caught my mouth in a hungry kiss and poked his tongue past my teeth as a low groan rumbled up from his chest.

I grabbed his shoulders and became lost in my dark world. His kiss was wild and untamed. It communicated passion, hunger and raw male desire. The added tobacco flavour, instead of repulsing me, enhanced the unwholesomeness of him that appealed to me so much.

He explored with his hands, dragging off my denim jacket and cupping my breasts through my short-sleeved top. The cupping turned into a squeeze, hard and firm, pressing my flesh into my chest.

I raked my fingers into his hair, let the warm, silken strands flow between my knuckles and urged him on. His body slammed into mine. A steely erection prodded my abdomen, and he reached down and slipped his hand between my legs, my short skirt no barrier to his determination.

'Liuz.' I curled my fingers into the waistband of his jeans that sat low on his hips. 'Please.'

'Ah, yes,' he said, stroking over my drenched thong, 'you are so ready for it.'

'I know, I want you, please, now.'

'And you're going to get it, but remember.' He sneaked a finger behind my gusset and stroked over my wet folds. 'Remember you came here tonight to be my slut, which means I get to say when and how you get fucked. Not you.'

I whimpered and allowed my knees to sink a little, wanting him to penetrate me with his fingers. I needed filling, by him.

Suddenly he stepped away, and once again circled my wrists with his hands. 'This way, slut, come this way.'

I stepped forwards, stumbling slightly in my heels. My knees quivered, lust a potent drug that had well and truly taken hold.

'Bend over,' he said, applying insistent pressure to the centre of my back.

Instinctively I reached forward. A smooth, flat surface lay before me – a table. The force on my back increased and I doubled until my chest and stomach hit the coolness and I was at a right angle.

'That's it, now spread your legs.'

His hands were all over me, my ass, behind the backs of my knees, round my ankles, pulling them wider. He wrapped something tight around my shins, binding me to the legs of the table.

I gripped the rim of the tabletop, my fingers like pincers. Sucked beads of sweat from my upper lip. A huge glut of pleasure soaked through me. I wasn't proud of the fact that blindfolded, bent double and getting tied to a table by a stranger was one of the sexiest things that had ever happened to me, but it was. There was no denying the overwhelming thrill bubbling in my guts at being prepared for a good fucking. It was off-the-scale horny.

Liuz stepped away. I twisted my head as if following his movements but could see nothing.

He was back, between my legs. I wriggled my ass and groaned in desperation as he shoved my skirt upwards, around my waist. His fingers, his cock, his mouth, anything would do.

'Keep still,' he said, yanking down my thong, partway to my knees, until it dug in and could go no further. 'Keep still. It's been a while since I've had a pussy to play with. I'm going to take my time.'

I rested my forehead on the table and shoved my bared bottom towards him; my action scraped the legs of the table on the floor. 'Please, Liuz, I –'

A sudden, sharp slap stung across my left buttock.

'Ow!'

'I said keep still.'

I bit down on my bottom lip as the pain streaked across my skin then bloomed to the surface, heating my flesh.

'Ah, *Aniolku*, you know I will give you what you need, so be a good girl for me. Be a good little slut.' His breath washed over my stinging ass – he was face-level with my throbbing clit and spread labial lips. I could only imagine the view he had of my asshole and my pussy, not to mention the ripe scent of my arousal that was wafting up to my own nose.

Finally he touched me, smoothed the tip of his finger through my folds, sought out my entrance and slid in.

I clenched around him and moaned appreciatively when he added another long finger.

'Ah, yes, so slutty and wet, you are such a rude girl, begging for my fingers. Well here, take more.'

The stretching increased significantly and his knuckles pressed up against my soft lips. He'd filled me quickly and I loved it. He began to wriggle inside me, industriously stroking over my sensitive spot then setting up a pumping in-and-out motion. Small sucking noises filled the air as I squelched around his digits.

'Ah, ah, ah.' I panted, reaching down and searching out my clit. I wanted to come, I wanted to come now, hard and fast, get the first one out the way so I could have more. I was greedy, greedy and needy.

'No,' he snapped. Another burning lick of pain scorched my buttock as he slapped me again. 'No, don't touch yourself. Keep fucking still.'

This time as the pain blossomed it settled in my abandoned clit, a hot fuzz of sensation that stimulated the nerves afresh.

He withdrew his fingers and in their place something cool nudged into me, just an inch. Not his cock, I didn't think.

'Condom,' I gasped.

He gave a snort of laughter. 'I don't think it's necessary just yet.' His voice came from above me – he was standing again.

Whatever he was inserting gained another inch. It had a generous girth, enough to fill my gaping, aching pussy quite nicely. I arched my back and relaxed my internal walls, keen to please him. Keen to take as much as I could.

'Ah, yes,' he said. 'That's it. Let it in.'

The insertion continued. The surface was smooth, and finally, when I couldn't accommodate any more, when the penetrating object hit my cervix, a long, low moan rumbled up from my chest and he stopped pressing it in.

'Yes, yes, *tak, tak*,' he said, 'Now you must stay like that.'

I lifted my head, my world still black, and clenched my full and fluttering pussy muscles.

'Now open your mouth.' He was in front of me.

I did as he asked.

As the scent of turned-on man, raw and heated, hit my nostrils, the smooth head of a cock brushed my lips. I chased for it, saliva pooling on my tongue. Oh, how I'd dreamed of tasting him. Night after night I'd imagined his flavour, his texture, the way he would fill every orifice I had.

'No, keep still.' He captured my head in his hands and held me firm. 'Open wide and take a deep breath. You said you wanted me to imagine your mouth was my hand and now that's going to be your reality.'

In one harsh thrust his meaty cock stuffed between my lips. The wide head slipped over my tongue to the back of my throat, and the thick shaft bulged my cheeks and pressed up onto my palate.

'Oh, fuck,' he groaned. His fingers tightened in my newly shortened hair, and he dug his nails into my scalp. 'You're gonna get it so good, so fucking good.'

He pulled out, then rammed back in. There was no finesse to his movements, no tenderness. He just set about fucking my mouth hard and fast and holding my head just where he wanted it.

'Yeah, I'm just using you to get off,' he gasped. 'So fucking slutty you don't even care, do you? You just want cock anyway you can get it. Cock in your mouth, your pussy, up your ass.'

I couldn't answer. My mouth was full, so was my pussy. As his cock hardened and drips of pre-cum lined my tongue, my cunt contracted. Whatever was in me was hard and cold and I would have done anything to have it pumping in and out the way his cock was pistoning into my mouth.

My jaw was so stretched it ached, and my breaths were hard to snatch around his thrusts. I didn't care. This was what I wanted.

'*Tak*, oh fuck, get ready for my spunk,' he groaned. 'No need for tissues, I'm going to flood your throat. Get ready to swallow, every last fucking drop until I tell you to stop, ah … ah … ah, yes.'

A guttural groan filled the room as his cum filled my mouth. I swallowed rapidly, gulping it down, hungry for more and sucking wildly. I wrapped my tongue around his pumping shaft and drew his glans as far down my throat as my gag reflex would allow.

'Ah, yes, *tak cholernie dobry*. Keep doing that, keep … doing … that.'

He rammed into me, his balls pressed against my chin and my nose buried in wiry pubic hair. More cum spurted into my mouth. I gagged, swallowed, gagged again. My heart was racing, my pussy contracting. I was so close to coming. Fellating Liuz was so damn exhilarating, and hearing his shouts of pleasure were such a colossal aphrodisiac that any discomfort I was feeling paled into insignificance.

'Yes, oh God, yes,' he said, finally loosening his grip on my hair. 'Stop now, stop sucking now.'

He withdrew and I pulled in much-needed oxygen. I was dizzy. Lights flashed behind my eyelids and my body felt floppy. But still my pussy hummed and my engorged clit throbbed.

'You suck dick well,' he said. I sensed him moving away from me, his body heat disappearing. 'I'm sure I will want to do that again, several times.'

'Yes,' I panted, 'but please.'

'You want to come too, don't you, my greedy little *Aniolku*?'

'Yes, I do. Now.'

'When I say.'

He was still breathless and I was aware of the foreign object inside me shifting. He gave it a few languid shunts that made me gasp then pulled it out.

'Here, open,' he said, pressing something against my mouth.

Was his cock hard again already?

'Eat.'

I let a cool, wet chunk of slipperiness into my mouth. It was definitely food. I bit into it and took a second to recognise the flavour of cucumber.

'More,' he said, pushing another segment into my mouth. He sounded like he, too, was munching.

I bit into it eagerly, grateful for the sweet, watery taste covering my dry tongue, though it was slightly musky too. Laced with a flavour I recognised but couldn't identify.

'You like?' he asked.

I nodded and opened my mouth.

He laughed and shoved more in. Juice dribbled down my chin, my mouth now brimming over. 'Can't get enough, can you?' he said, moving back behind me.

I wiped a hand over my wet face, slurping and licking my lips.

'You have a slut's pussy,' he said, stroking over my engorged folds. 'Slutty and needy, it takes anything. I can tell.'

It took all my willpower to resist shoving my hand down to fret my clit. I needed to climax so badly it was fuddling my thoughts.

But it was several, long, agonising minutes before he touched me again. 'Here, take my dick in your pussy.'

With one devastating thrust he burrowed in.

I cried out. His cock was long and steel-hard again.

Whatever had just been inside me, as I'd sucked him off, had barely prepared me for Liuz's monster dick.

As I struggled to take his length and girth, sweat pricked over me and my pulse thudded loud in my ears. I wailed again as he pulled halfway out then shoved in once more.

'Be quiet, slut,' he hissed angrily.

I mashed my lips together and braced for his next thrust. It came, hard and swift, barging over my G-spot with deadly accuracy.

My mound was rubbing on the hard surface of the table, enough to stimulate. It combined with the growing pressure the fast and furious sensations his cock was creating deep within my pussy. Soon an orgasm would be mine. The tightening in my belly and the trembling in my pelvis warned me. Juices flooded from me; finally, I was getting the fucking I needed.

I moaned and groaned, revelled in the build-up to climax and briefly wondered what I must look like. Bent over, bound, blindfolded and being fucked harshly, so harshly. I imagined my skin pale against his olive tones, my lack of body hair a shocking contrast to his hair-coated limbs and chest.

Suddenly it was there. My orgasm claimed me with a swiftness that surprised me. It must have been the lewd images in my head that had rocketed it out of control. My whole body tightened, as if my nerve endings were stretched to the limit. A huge ball of pleasure that caused my feet to lift from the floor and my hips to shove back for more, raged through me.

'Yes, yes, take my dick,' he shouted, then meshed his fingers into my hair, above the tie of the blindfold, and pulled. Hard. 'Take all of my dick.'

'Ah, ah,' I called out, bliss and agony twisting together as my back and neck were snapped upwards.

He didn't ease his tormenting; he kept pulling wickedly.

'This was how you wanted it, remember,' he said, pounding into me, over and over.

'Yes, yes,' I said, riding through blissful waves of ecstasy and not caring about my arched spine and my abused hair roots. 'Yes, oh fuck, Liuz, yes, yes.'

He groaned long and loud. His thighs slapped against the backs of mine. The legs of the table shifted and banged as his tempo increased even more. I was pulsating, writhing. Stuffed full of his dick. My orgasm was wreaking havoc, it wasn't abating; instead, it was rolling up again, preparing for another assault on my G-spot.

'So fucking filthy, you're a whore,' he groaned. 'You're my whore.' He slapped down hard on my buttock and his palm sent pain whistling through my nerve endings.

Jerking forwards, I reached behind myself, as if to protect my ass from another slap. But I didn't want to be saved, not really, and when he hit again I allowed the dark, red-hot pleasure to spread. As it did I twisted and twitched. Another orgasm swept through me, just as violent as the first, and I cried out. The release almost sent me delirious. All that existed were the waves of wild satisfaction claiming me.

Finally Liuz tensed. '*Tak*, oh fuck, you're milking me so damn hard,' he groaned as he erupted. Then he froze, buried deep, let go of my head, gripped my hips, and shunted in some more. It was as though he wouldn't be happy until he was nudging up against my diaphragm. 'Ah, yes ... yes.'

I gasped for oxygen, let my head fall to the table and my back flatten out. My pussy was convulsing, gripping his cock. As my mind came back to me and the giddy heights of ecstasy retreated, I knew that it had, undoubtedly, been the most intense, exquisite orgasm of my life.

When could I have another?

Chapter Five

I heard him move away, a shuffle of feet on floor, and as I caught my breath I imagined him standing with his back to the window, taking in the sight of me sprawled like this. I could see it for myself, my mind full of the image, and my sex spasmed with the thrill of it. Would he leave me here, waiting, anticipating his next move? Or would he untie me, take off the blindfold and allow me to look at him for what he thought was the first time? The not knowing was all part of the excitement – excitement that seemed to have no thought of stopping. It barrelled through me, adrenaline on wings, and I sucked in a deep breath in order to calm myself. My chest hurt from the rapid beating of my heart, lungs painfully filling then emptying.

This man did things to my body without even having to touch it.

He was close, his breathing steadying now, but not close enough for me to feel his body heat. Time went slowly, as though I was suspended, where the world had stopped and fate was deciding where to take us next. I wanted him again, wanted him inside me, his hands all over me. My skin hummed with the need for his touch. Still gripping the table edge, I lifted my face, raised my body, the whole of me wrung out and unsteady. He'd reduced me to exactly what I'd wanted him to – a fatigued mess who was more than ready to be used and abused again.

He could do anything he wanted and I wouldn't mind. That stop word – I wouldn't be using it.

A smudge of sound had me holding my breath, then a creak of floorboards. I sensed him coming closer, and the hairs on my arms bristled at his approach. Was he ready for me again? So soon? Was that what he'd been doing? Jerking himself back to hardness? I held my breath, tightening my hold on the table, and waited for him to ram inside me without warning.

He didn't.

The sharp trilling of a phone jangled my nerves, and Liuz sighed. The ringing stopped, and he spoke in rapid Polish, his tone angry. A slap to a piece of furniture had me tensing, pressing my fingertips into the underside of the table. Although I'd been speaking to him for a long time online, I didn't know him, not really. That had been the attraction, the thrill, meeting up with a man who was potentially dangerous and had the ability to harm me, with no one knowing a damn thing about it unless I chose to tell them. I was here, though, at his bedsit, and that had to count for something. He wouldn't risk doing anything too bad because I knew where he lived. I could have told someone where I would be tonight, for all he knew. No, he wouldn't take his anger out on me.

A snap brought me back to the here and now – the phone closing?

'That is all for tonight, you dirty bitch.'

His words didn't make sense, and I frowned. We were supposed to spend all night together, weren't we? He was meant to pleasure me until I couldn't stand, couldn't even walk out of here. I would stay the night, curled up beside him in his bed, and leave in the morning, my clothes and the state of me leaving no doubt in people's minds as to what I'd been doing the night before.

'What?' I said, my throat dry, legs going to jelly. If my heart beat any faster I thought I might be sick.

'I said, that is all for tonight.'

I knew what he'd bloody said, but this wasn't how it was supposed to be! 'What? No, we'd planned on me staying here. You were going to fuck me all night. I came here thinking –'

'The wrong thing, *Aniolku*. Did I ever make these promises? Did I ever write them down? Did I say that tonight you would stay?'

'No, but –'

'Then it was what you had assumed. Never take things for granted, Hannah. You said you wanted to come here and be my slut. That is what has happened. Nothing more and nothing less.'

I was confused, so damn confused my frown hurt my head. The blindfold hurt too, tied as tight as it was, a steel band that made the skin around it throb. What had happened to make him change? He wanted me to stay; he still had more fucking energy in him, I could tell. So why did I need to go home? I knew I sounded like a whiny female, but God, I'd waited so long for this. It wasn't fair that my fantasy was going to get cut short.

'So this is it? I go home now? You've fucked me so now I leave?'

'I've fucked you, as we planned I would. Yes, this is it. For now.'

I wanted to embrace what he'd said – *for now* – and loved the idea of me returning here whenever he instructed, him fucking me in bite-sized episodes. But at the same time, my idea of being pummelled all night wasn't going to happen, and I didn't think I could process it fully right now. I'd pinned all my hopes on it. Damn, it was what I thought he'd wanted too. That phone call had cut short our plans, that was it. If he'd never gotten that call, I'd be staying here, I was sure of it.

His voice deepened, became harder, as if re-confirming our relationship. 'You are nothing but a slutty whore,

61

here for me to use whenever I want. Whores do not call the shots. Whores come running when they are told, ready to spread their legs for payment. Your payment was orgasms. You ask no questions when you are here with me. Online is a different matter. This is how it is with us, *Aniolku*. I thought you knew that.'

'I did, I do, but I thought –'

'I will untie you now. You will keep the blindfold on until you have left my place. I will email again.'

'When?' I asked, panic seeping into me.

What if this was it? What if he was lying and never intended contacting me again? Now he'd fucked me, I was more hooked on him than ever. I wouldn't allow this to be a one-time thing. No damn way. If he thought to just brush me off, then, God, I could be a bitch if I wanted.

'When I feel like it,' he said.

When he felt like it? He was letting me know he was the boss, no doubt about it. I wasn't in any way allowed to make decisions while here. It was him, all him. I'd liked the idea of that before I'd met him, before he'd done things to me tonight no other had done, no other had made me feel, and I was hungry for more. Greedier than any other time in my life for the touch of a man. And not just any man, either. It had to be him. I was hooked, I knew that, unashamedly hooked.

The bindings on my legs loosened then fell away, leaving the site of where they'd been numb. He was sure not to touch me, and there I was, wishing with every bit of me that his skin would brush mine, that I'd get that zing through my veins and tingles all over my body when he did. Feeling absurdly lost and bereft, I stood upright, patting down my body to draw up my thong. I pulled down my skirt, then reached up to remove the blindfold.

'Do *not* take that off. I told you: keep it on until you leave my place. I do not want to say this, Hannah, but if you cannot obey me, I will be forced to say the stop word. I do not screw disobedient women. It would be a shame to find out now that you are just like most others, a girl who cannot take instruction and wants to rule everything. You said you were not like that, that you wanted me to dominate you and actualise your fantasies. Did you lie to me?'

My heart sank along with my stomach. 'No, I didn't lie. I'm sorry. I'll do whatever you say. It's just that I wan–'

I stopped myself from doing exactly what he'd just said he didn't want. Whining. Wanting more than he was prepared to give. Taking a deep breath through my nose, telling myself to just do as I was told and leave the room, I stretched my hands out in order to find the door. He gripped my wrist, firm but not too rough, and led the way.

'This is the exciting bit,' he said, thumb rubbing circles on my inner wrist. 'This is where you get to feel like a real whore. You leave, you walk down the street, and you wait at the bus stop with other people staring at you, knowing you have just been fucked. You stink of sex. You look dishevelled. Is that not what you wanted?'

I agreed that it was, but the sting of being thrown out like this when I'd wanted so much more…

It didn't matter what I wanted. It was all about what he wanted. I was his slut.

I nodded.

'Good girl. Here is your bag.' He pressed the strap into my hand. 'Now go. I have things I must do.'

Things more important than me. I clenched my teeth. Stop it, I told myself. Stop being such a … a needy woman! It's not who you are when you are here.

He pushed me in the back, and I stumbled forwards, arms outstretched ready to brace a fall. I didn't smack into anything and regained my balance, the quiet click of his door closing the last indication that he'd meant what he'd said. I was going home. I lifted my hands, tugged off the blindfold, and stood facing the main door to the street, blinking, unable, for a moment, to take in what had just happened. I'd been fucked well and good, but here I stood, cast away like some nasty piece of rubbish. I was nothing more than a prostitute tonight, just like he'd said. I'd wanted that earlier, wanted to experience what it was like so much, and it had been wonderful, but now? Dare I say I was falling for him, or at least falling for the way he made me feel? I knew obsession and love were two completely different things, but weren't they two sides of the same coin? Who said you couldn't love someone and be obsessed with them at the same time?

It stung that I stood out here, a probable mess to look at, here for anyone to see should they come out of their bedsits. They might look at me with pity. Who knew how many times Liuz had done this? How many times he'd shoved a woman out the door with the promise of an email 'when he felt like it'.

Suddenly something inside me fell into place. I realised I was happy to be used as a slut but I wasn't about to be cast aside like this. Oh, I'd play his game all right, acting as though I was doing what he told me and taking all the deliciously depraved pleasure he could give me, but I'd also make him depend on me. I'd make him want me and need me the way I did him. I'd do that if it was the last thing I did. I was going to make it so that if I wasn't around, he'd miss me, want me, need me.

Mind made up, I straightened, hung the blindfold on his handle, and walked towards the main door, deliberately not looking back at his. I'd accepted them but I didn't like the new feelings inside me, ones that spoke of me wanting more than just fucks with him. That wasn't how this had started; it wasn't how it was meant to pan out.

I admitted, as I swung open the door and the night air clutched at my bare legs, that I had fallen foul of the one thing some men detested in a woman. Subconsciously, I had wanted a relationship, a relationship that was more than the one we currently had. When had that changed? When had me just wanting any fuck he offered, whenever he offered it, become not enough?

The minute he sunk his cock inside me, that's when.

Angry at myself, I hoisted my bag strap onto my shoulder, shut the door and began the walk to the bus stop. This pipe dream of mine had to stop. I couldn't be doing with a serious relationship anyway. They hadn't worked in the past, what with my job taking me out at all hours sometimes, chasing scoops and hoping to catch a break on the biggest story London had ever seen. No, what Liuz offered was perfect. He'd cater for my dirty fantasies whenever it suited us both. I'd just expected a longer time with him tonight, that was all. But it was OK, because I'd use him like he was using me. I'd let him think he didn't care for me, but by the time we were done – if we were ever done – he'd wish he'd never said the stop word. One thing was for sure, I knew damn well I would never say 'Kilimanjaro'.

As I sat on the cold metal of the bus stop seat, a woman with her young son gave me a filthy look and moved away to stand on the other side of the rain shelter. I thought about what I must look like, lipstick smeared, hair a mess from being tugged. And Liuz had said I stunk of sex. That it was obvious what I'd been doing.

Maybe I looked like a real prostitute.

I didn't care.

Ignoring the woman, I stared up the street at house windows lit from within, at lampposts emitting amber glows that splashed onto the pavement beneath. I rubbed my arms and shivered a little from the cold. Yes, this was how a prostitute would feel, all hunched up in a bus shelter, bare legs pimpled with goose bumps, nipples hard and hurting from the biting autumn weather.

If this was how Liuz wanted me to feel, then I would feel it as part of the game.

If this was how our relationship was to be, then I'd take it, with my own private terms kept firmly in my head, a secret.

I was too far gone on him to back out now. Too obsessed with him to allow the small matter of staying the whole night to upset the balance.

Mind more settled now I was back on track, I squinted into the distance to wait for the first sign of the bus that would take me home. I'd slipped my return ticket into my skirt pocket earlier and stood now to check it was still there. It wasn't. It must have fallen out as Liuz fucked me. Landed on his floor. Had he found it? Was he holding it now, thinking of what we'd done? Or had that damn phone call taken his whole attention? There were things he had to do, he'd said. What were they? Just what the hell could have made him angry enough to cut short our night?

I was determined to find out what was important to Liuz.

The bus appeared down the street, coming closer with a slight sway, the top deck empty, only two people occupying the lower. It stopped with a hiss and the sliding open of doors, and I waited for the woman and her child to board first. As I stepped on, she shuffled up the aisle, seating her son then sitting beside him, a mother's instinct protecting him from my taint, what I was.

I paid the fare and took the stairs, sitting at the front so I could better see when my stop approached. The last thing I needed tonight was to miss it. I wanted to go home now, to check if Liuz had emailed already, to get back to our normal pattern. One I knew well. One that made me feel safe. I didn't like how I'd felt back there, needy and out of control. Maybe that was his intention, to wear me down until I couldn't function without him. I was a strong woman; he knew that from our emails. Maybe he liked the idea of turning a usually self-assured girl into a begging wreck.

However much that appealed to me, a journey where I'd lose myself bit by bit, I knew I wouldn't be able to stand it. I'd play the game, if that was the way he wanted it, but I'd still be in control.

Was that what I really believed? The way I felt about him, the way I went off on tangents just at the thought of him?

I knew I'd become fixated the moment I'd decided to go to Brixton and spy on him. Knew it when I painted him on my wall and spread those pictures of him on the floor. It was irrational, not the usual way women behaved – not any women I knew, anyway. If I was honest, I was well aware of how this would look to someone else, to me at one time long ago – before Liuz, before those filthy emails – but at the same time I didn't care. He swam in my veins, had burrowed deep inside me, and I was damned if I'd let him go without a fight. Do as I was told, exactly as I'd been told. I couldn't imagine not having him in my life now. No more emails. No more fucking. Now this new phase had started, I couldn't risk it being taken away. I wanted more of his cock inside me, and if it meant I could only have it every so often, then so be it.

My stop came, so I got off the bus and headed for home, safe in the knowledge that if anyone I knew saw me they wouldn't think I was me anyway. Not with this hair, these clothes. They'd realise who I was eventually, of course they would, but for tonight I was safe to slip inside and mull over what had happened in the past hour or so.

I went straight for the mural and stood staring at it while memories filled my head and sexual excitement set my clit to throbbing. I dropped my bag to the floor and walked forward, brushing my fingertips over the painted cock I yet had the privilege of seeing for real. The way it had felt as it jammed in and out of me somehow matched the way I had painted it. I leaned forward, pressed my nose to it, and inhaled deeply. Wishing I could smell it. Wishing that when I dashed out my tongue I'd be met with soft skin encasing hardness, not a cold wall that yielded nothing.

I stepped back, semi-appalled at what I'd just done. I glanced about, as though someone was here to witness my act; then rushed over to the window to snap the curtains closed. I felt across my desk for the lamp and switched it on; staring at the mural now lit a muted yellow. This man, God, he'd wormed his way inside me, and now that I'd had him, his hands touching places I'd only dreamed and hoped he would, I wasn't letting him go for anyone or anything. So what if I was a little fanatical? I wasn't hurting anyone. He would never say the stop word, I'd make sure of that.

Chapter Six

The following day, I called the office early, feigning sickness. I wasn't lying, when I thought about it. I was sick, just not ill. Sick with wanting Liuz. I said I'd be OK tomorrow, back out in the field in search of good stories, and the editor had sighed. There wasn't much he could do about my absence, really. I was freelance. I just had to hope I stumbled on a good story soon, otherwise he might drop me, decline future stories I submitted, and I didn't think my landlord would appreciate having to wait for his rent until I earned more money.

I hadn't slept too well, annoyed to hell and back Liuz hadn't sent an email last night, not even a thank you or 'Sleep tight'. I felt a huge dose of the grumps coming on, feelings of rejection swamping me whole, and pressed my lips together so tight I imagined they'd gone white.

'I'm not going down that road,' I said to the mural, pulling a dressing gown around myself. 'You're not going to turn me into a needy, simpering wreck. I'm going to make you want me so much you can't think, can't breathe.'

It was all very well me saying that out loud, but could I really do it? Liuz was a strong man, in body and in mind, and I doubted very much he would be easy to break. But everyone had a chink in their armour, didn't they? Everyone had an Achilles heel. I just had to find his. Once again it came to my mind – what was important to him?

I thudded into my office, booted up the laptop then went in search of coffee. When I came back, my palm curled around a steaming mug, I checked my mail. My heartbeat kicked up a notch.

There was mail from Liuz, and to my surprise there was an attachment.

I gnawed at the inside of my cheek as I waited for the message to open.

'Hey, Aniolku. I have sent you a present to remind you of our wonderful evening together, though you must tell me exactly how it makes you feel, for as you know I am eager to learn more about how to best realise your fantasies.'

My stomach clenched as I opened the attachment. It was a video, and instantly I recognised the setting. The dull, dishwater colours, the single bare bulb overhead and one table with thin legs standing in the middle. It could only be Liuz's room.

From my speakers there was a sudden knocking and Liuz, with his back to me, stood and moved to the door.

Of course I knew what he looked like, but still, the image of his long, golden back, shirtless and disappearing into those worn jeans, had my stomach clenching with desire. I sat heavily on my chair and turned up the volume on my computer.

He opens the door and I spot a section of my face beyond his shoulder. My mouth flattened nervously and the big, painted-on eyes on the blindfold look comical and creepy all at the same time.

He grabs my wrists, and my lips part in surprise as I'm tugged into the room and the door shuts. My bag falls to the floor.

He speaks in a low murmur and I reply. His hands fiddle with the tightness of the material bound around my head. My scalp prickles now at the memory and instinctively I smooth my hair over the crown of my head.

Still I can't see his face, but I remember our conversation about the stop word. I hear myself repeat 'Kilimanjaro' as my chin is caught in his big hand. His head dips and I know he is kissing me, hot and hard. I remember his taste, smoky and sinful, infused with potent maleness. I lick my lips, seeking for a lingering trace of his flavour. Of course, I don't find it.

His hands roam my body, and I mesh my fingers in his hair. Sitting in my office now, I can't help but tweak my clit through my pyjama pants and my breaths catch in my throat. This is even better than I could have ever imagined. He'd caught our whole, seedy encounter on film. This was going to be masturbation fodder for years to come.

'This way, slut, come this way.'

Oh, how I loved his voice and the way he spoke to me.

I stumble forward and he walks, back to the camera, right up to the table. When he reaches it I see how the angle of the lens is set low, so that when I bend over I'm the main part of the frame. The top of the screen stops just above his nipples. His facial features have still not graced the image he's sent me.

'That's it, now spread your legs.'

I do as he asks without hesitation. A small part of me knows I should feel ashamed, dirty, but I don't. Instead, I watch with fascination as he binds me to the table, his arms and busy fingers securing me for his ministrations. I know what's coming next, but still, excitement buzzes through me.

Although the light is dim I can make out the whiteness of my fingernails as I clutch the rim of the table, my head turning as I try and follow Liuz's movements through the sounds he makes – his clothes, his footsteps, his breaths.

He's back between my legs. I'm wriggling and groaning.

'Keep still.' He yanks at my thong. 'Keep still. It's been a while since I've had a pussy to play with. I'm going to take my time.'

'Please, Liuz, I —'

A sudden sharp slap snaps from the screen. I jolt in my chair, remembering the sting across my left buttock. It comes back now, a sizzling sensation my nerves are loath to forget.

'Ow!'

'Ah, *Aniolku*, you know I will give you what you need, so be a good girl for me. Be a good little slut.'

His face is just out of shot when finally he slides his fingers into my pussy.

'Ah, yes, so slutty and wet, you are such a rude girl, begging for my fingers. Well here, take more.'

I watched, fascinated as his hand and fingers appear and disappear between my legs. Squelching noises add to the erotic image and I can't help but wish I was back there, feeling him doing it to me all over again.

'No, don't touch yourself. Keep fucking still.' He withdraws his fingers, steps away for the briefest of moments. Then he is back, holding something long and dark green.

It's the damn cucumber he fed me.

'Condom,' I gasp.

He laughs. 'I don't think it's necessary just yet.'

Where his fingers had entered me moments ago, now the cucumber presses forward. I arch my back, raise my chin to the ceiling, my jaw slack. My unseeing eyes stare at the camera. Soon the cucumber is more than halfway into my pussy and I'm panting and my body is still and tense.

He moves in front of me, his torso slipping between me and the lens for a split second like a black shadow.

Then I see his beautiful cock for the first time. He's holding it in his hand, his palm lazily smoothing up and down the erect shaft. The head is thick and domed. A deep, finger-sized trench circles the glans and his slit is large, the colour of blood.

'Now open your mouth.'

I do as he asks but jerk my neck when his cock brushes my lips.

'No, keep still.' He grabs for my head, blocking out some of the image with his long, hair-coated forearms. 'Open wide and take a deep breath. You said you wanted me to imagine your mouth was my hand and now that's going to be your reality.'

He shunts in. My body jars then braces. The cucumber bobs as I clench around it.

'Oh, fuck. You're gonna get it so good, so fucking good.'

He sets up a wild rhythm, hissing obscenities at me as he thrusts. Before long his climax claims him. I see myself struggling: for air and not to choke on his cum.

'You suck dick well.' He releases my head, withdraws and moves away.

I know what's coming next.

The damn cucumber.

A tirade of emotions tumble through me as I watch him fuck me with the long fruit, then pull it out and, with a small pen knife, he chops off chunks which he then feeds to me.

I gobble it up, greedy for the moistness on my tongue. I see him lift slivers up and out of the frame, toward his own mouth.

I'm eating the very thing that had just penetrated my pussy. It's coated in my creamy desire. I had no clue about it at the time. I just wanted everything he gave me.

He is back behind me, his dick hard and thankfully sheathed in a condom.

With one devastating thrust he gains entry. I cry out on the screen. In my office I gasp. It was a brutally fast and hard penetration, but it gave me such exquisite pleasure.

He tells me to be quiet. I moan a response. He grabs my hair and pulls my neck and spine into an unnatural position. Pistons in and out of me like a man possessed.

Then, for the first time ever, I watch myself climax.

My entire body tightens. My feet and toes lift off the floor as much as their binds will allow and my hips snap back for more depth. My hands grip the table and my mouth opens wide. With each pound my breasts shunt forward, the soft flesh jiggling and my nipples straining beneath the material of my top.

I call out. It's a wild, guttural noise that could be interpreted as extreme discomfort or ecstatic pleasure.

He carries on fucking me. 'This was how you wanted it, remember.'

'Yes, yes.'

His deep groan mixes with the sound of his thighs slapping onto the backs of mine.

'So fucking filthy, you're a whore.'

He hits my buttock with the palm of his hand. A fast blur of light on the screen. I jerk away then cry out as another orgasm besieges me.

Finally Liuz comes. '*Tak*, oh fuck, you're milking me so damn hard.'

As I watch him stiffen and put all his considerable muscle into ramming his dick forward, another small orgasm grabs me now. I lift my ass from the office chair. The image before me and the stimulation of my finger pressing against the seam of my pants is enough to create a tight little climax that drags a gasp from my chest.

The screen freezes on an image of me with my face twisted towards the camera. My mouth is open loosely as I pant for breath and pinch the table. Those damn drawn-on, unblinking eyes mock me.

I give a shaky sigh and close the attachment. But not before saving it into a special folder.

I hit reply.

'Morning, Liuz. Thank you for the present, it was very thoughtful of you. Watching you fuck my pussy made me hot and wet all over again.' I paused, wondering how to word the rest of the email. 'I especially liked sucking your dick, how you held my head and spurted your thick spunk down my throat. You said you wanted to do it again, several times – when?'

I hit send. Instantly, I regretted the last word. It was so needy, so demanding, exactly what I'd said I wouldn't be. But what could I do about it? I *was* needy. So needy that I didn't think I could breathe let alone function without seeing him again today.

'I have important business to tend to this afternoon. Perhaps tonight we could explore your slutty tendencies further.'

My heart soared and a bubble of triumph lurched through me. It was just as I had thought. He hadn't done fucking me last night. He did still want me. Wanted to bury his dick in my slutty pussy.

'I'm working to a deadline,' I typed back. 'Got an editor breathing down my neck. So I'm not sure if I'll be able to make it.' I hit send and congratulated myself on my nonchalant response.

'You will,' he replied instantaneously.

* * *

Quickly, dressed in jeans, a thick black sweater, and boots that would keep me dry if the clouds had a mind to release rain on me again, I wound a dark-grey scarf around my neck and the lower half of my face, and then jammed on a matching beanie hat. As the sun was shining despite the time of year, I wouldn't look too out of place wearing sunglasses, but even if I did, I couldn't risk being spotted. Not when I was going to stake out Liuz's place and follow him if he left his flat to attend to his *important business*. I was a pro at this, could stand or sit in the shadows for hours if I had to. He'd come out eventually, and even if I had to wait until nightfall, I'd do it.

With sandwiches for lunch, a cold salad for dinner, and my camera packed inside my rucksack, plus snacks and drinks to keep hunger at bay in between meals, I left my place and headed for the bus stop. I had a purpose and was smug to note my stride was no-nonsense, that I must look as though, if approached, I'd bite someone's head off. The burn of his arrogant 'You will' was giving me the courage and determination to see this through. I wanted to find information about Liuz, have something on him that I could whip out and slap him with if the time came that he made it clear he'd finished playing with me.

He'd stop playing with me when I said so, and only then.

The bus arrived in a short time, trundling along as though overburdened by the many passengers it carried. I'd left my place when people would be travelling to work; all the better to blend in with the crowd. I peered through the windows as the doors opened with a feral hiss, seeing that I'd have to stand and hold the handrail on my journey to Brixton. That was OK, I could deal with anything the mood I was in.

Once on the bus, I wedged myself between an over-weight businessman who smelled like day's-old body odour, and a spindly woman who looked like she'd fall over if the wind decided to blow on her. It wasn't the best of journeys, but needs must. I had one day to complete this mission and dig up information before reality set in and I returned to doing my real job.

At the stop close to Liuz's house, I stepped off the bus and walked down his street, careful to keep close to the fences and gates outside the properties. Just past his flat was a wide-trunked oak, broad enough for me to hide behind, and a line of cars parked close to the kerb. As I passed his window on the left, I glanced the other way, ensuring he'd only see the back of my head should he happen to be looking out onto the street. I had a rough idea of the times he was at home from the email conversations we'd had, and he was definitely a creature of habit. He would be home now, and in around an hour he would go out, or, if he didn't go out, he worked or did whatever the hell he did because his emails usually stopped. They started again two hours later, so I prepared myself for a bit of a wait until he left his flat.

Situating myself behind the oak, I pressed against it and peered around the side. I had the perfect view of his window and the bushes beneath. I could only hope the neighbours around here weren't the kind to telephone the police to report a loiterer. I really didn't need that. I eyed the area and realised no one would give much of a shit about me being out here squashed against a tree. Each house appeared to be the same as the one Liuz lived in, all with multiple bell buttons beside the front doors. I suspected students and single people occupied the premises.

I wasted about half an hour scoping the street, noting alleys between houses I could duck down if I needed to make myself scarce. Many had chest-high refuse bins backed up to the walls, and that suited me just fine. I could crouch beside them and be totally out of sight. I nodded, pleased that my surroundings were in line with any eventuality that might crop up, and swung my rucksack off my shoulder in order to pull out an apple. Eating would waste another ten minutes or so – that's if I could stomach it. My heart rate had picked up as thoughts of Liuz leaving his home weaved through my mind.

I could do this. I did this kind of thing all the time. I just happened to be intent on following someone who might recognise me and wonder what the hell I was doing following him. Breaking the rules.

My sunglasses pinched the bridge of my nose. Reluctant to take them off but unable to stand the irritation, I stuck them in my jacket pocket. I bit into the green apple. Juice squirted out and hit me in the eye. I stifled a squeal and bunched my eyes shut, rubbing the sting away with my knuckles. I should have kept the bloody glasses on. I chewed and swallowed, my appetite for eating suddenly gone, and opened my eyes to look around for a nearby rubbish bin. To my right, a dog waste bin hung lopsided from a lamppost, but the good citizen in me wouldn't allow for dumping my apple in there. I hunkered down and opened my bag, rummaging about for one of the spare sandwich bags I'd packed. Putting the apple inside and securing my rucksack, I stood upright and swung it onto my back before looking over at Liuz's window.

He was staring out. Right at me.

Shit! No sunglasses!

I jumped. Surely he couldn't see me here behind the tree. Only part of one eye was showing, a sliver of the side of my face. Nerves dancing in my belly, I eased right out of sight, put my glasses back on, and inhaled deeply. It was OK. He hadn't seen me, I was sure of it. And if he had, it wouldn't look like me anyway. I'd purposely dressed unladylike. I could be one of many students who undoubtedly lived in these parts, a wacky one who thought nothing of standing behind trees with their day's meals in their rucksack.

With that thought in mind, I inched my face to the side again. Liuz wasn't at the window, and I sighed out my relief. Then sprang back in alarm as he breezed past me down the street, head bent low, hands in black jacket pockets. The jacket hem covered his ass, but I still imagined the swell of it beneath, how it would look, snugly encased in dark denim. Preoccupied with gawping at him, I lost concentration and my foot slipped off the curb behind me, stuck fast between the curb and a car tyre. My ankle twisted. I bit down on my bottom lip to stop myself screeching from the sharp pain and turned to watch him walking away. He strode at a pretty fast clip, and I needed to get my foot free fast if I were to keep up with him before he went out of sight.

Steeling myself for more pain, I wiggled my foot loose and tested how my weight felt on my ankle. It wasn't too bad, so I lightly limped after him, keeping a good distance so that if he looked back I could slink out of sight down an alley. He reached the end of the road; then glanced left and right before crossing over the intersection ahead. I pursued, adrenaline swirling through me at the thought of finally finding out something different about him.

We walked through the streets until he took a left at some wastelands and tromped over rough grass that reached his knees in places. On the other side stood some warehouses, not abandoned by the look of them but very much in use. I hesitated to follow, because if he glanced over his shoulder now, I'd be fully exposed. What else was I supposed to do, though? I'd have to take the risk.

I reached halfway across the wastelands and started to breathe a little easier, thanking God or whoever happened to give a damn that he hadn't snuck a glance behind him. He still had his head bent and hands in his pockets, as though he was so deep in thought he wouldn't hear the rustle of the grass as I tried to walk quietly anyway. What was on his mind?

Another couple of minutes' walk saw him entering the site of the warehouses. He clearly knew where he was going, because he lifted his head and strode with purpose, shoulders straight, hands now swinging by his sides. I drew up behind him as close as I dared, not wanting to get lost in this rabbit warren of pathways between buildings.

He walked up to a grey steel effort with red-painted double doors. Before entering, he looked left and right again, appearing up to no good in my eyes. I'd seen this kind of behaviour before when trailing some drug dealers. They all did that left-to-right thing, and they all rolled their shoulders before entering a building, just like Liuz was doing now.

The door closed behind him with a loud clang, and I waited a few seconds before pushing it open. Slowly. Who knew what lay behind those doors? A wide open space where I'd be seen easily or a small office with some woman sitting behind the desk I'd have to explain myself to? I couldn't think about that now; I'd deal with whatever presented itself to me once I stepped inside.

Do it. Go in.

I obeyed my inner voice and eased inside. Bright halogen lights illuminated the place, making me squint from the glare. Cardboard boxes, taped closed, stood in stacks, creating aisles in between, right down to the far wall. Closer to me, some were open, white polystyrene beans hiding the contents. To my right, a dirty, rusty steel shelving unit around six-foot wide and just as tall held more boxes, smaller ones with no labels that could hold anything from knick-knacks to mobile phones. It was clearly a storage unit, although where the hell Liuz had gone was anyone's guess.

I stepped forward cautiously, nerves biting my innards, my hands shaking just a little. I was nervous, no denying it, but curiosity prompted me to walk down one of the aisles. The boxes either side of me were stacked so high I couldn't see over the top, which thankfully meant if Liuz was on the other side he couldn't see me. The problem was, the aisles were pretty long, so I risked being seen if he walked across either end. I tiptoed on, each step measured and careful so I didn't create any noise. I couldn't afford to make even the quietest of scuffles.

At the end, I blew out my breath and peered right. A slim aisle ran to the far wall, nothing of interest to see. To my left was the same sight except for a partially open door at the end. Light spilled out of the gap and drew me towards it. I crept, conscious that even my breathing was too loud. The low murmur of voices reached me, two males, one of them definitely Liuz. My pulse thudded in my ears, and I had that horrible feeling in my stomach that I should get out of here pretty damn quick. My instincts screamed for me to turn around and go back the way I had come, to run across the wastelands and jump on a bus that would take me home. But a journalist never backed out, never balked at the first sign of a few nerves; so I continued on until I reached the end. I settled myself in the corner, able to see through the gap in the door.

An office of sorts lay beyond. The corner of a cheap wooden desk and an equally cheap, listing bookcase behind it brought to mind every warehouse office I'd ever seen on TV: sparse, walls of bare plaster, the room not designed for comfort but functionality. I couldn't see Liuz or whoever he was talking to. Their conversation was muted, a rumble of sound that gave me the impression they were conscious they might be overheard. I guessed that workers perhaps came in and out of here at any given time and the men in the office had to be careful.

Just my luck to get caught by one of them.

I strained my ears, eager to pick up any snippet I could, eager to learn more about the man I obsessed over. I cursed myself for not pulling out my camera earlier, but then again, maybe that was a good thing. The shutter going off, if I managed to get a good shot, would alert them to my presence. And who was to say there was anything worth taking a picture of anyway?

'I told you,' Liuz said, raising his voice. 'I do not have it.'

'And I told you,' another man said, voice a broad Cockney accent full of menace, 'that if you didn't have it by today, you'd have to give me something of monetary equivalence.'

Liuz chuckled, the sound rough and with a slight edge that made me think he wasn't actually laughing in the laughing sense. 'I do not have anything worth that amount, you know this.'

'Then you shouldn't have entered the deal.'

The deal? What the hell was going on?

'I thought the person who I was going to sell to was solid,' Liuz said. 'I did not expect him to back out.'

'Much like I didn't expect this from you. So now we both know how the other feels, yeah?'

That other voice was heavy with danger, and I swallowed to wet my suddenly dry throat. Inching forward, I stared through the crack between the door and jamb, making out a high window, sunlight streaming through it to shine on a beefcake of a man standing in a black leather jacket, tight black jeans, and not a strand of hair on his gangster-type head. He looked to be about thirty-five, all brawn and attitude. My God, I didn't know what was the matter with me lately, but he sent my knees weak. He was dodgy, I knew that just by looking at him, and the way he stared ahead, presumably at Liuz, with a cold, beady-eyed black stare, had me sucking in a breath.

'When did he back out?' Beefcake asked, pulling his hands out of his pockets and examining the gun he held as though it was nothing more than a toy.

My stomach rolled and bile rose into my throat, coating the back of my tongue. Bloody hell! I was well and truly stuck between a rock and a hard place here, my need to know what was going on keeping me in place but my instincts screaming for me to get the hell out and run for the hills.

'Last night,' Liuz said. 'By telephone.'

'Ah, the worst kind of bloke,' Beefcake said. 'I suppose I should be grateful you at least turned up here to tell me to my face.' He looked around then at the high ceiling, placing the gun in one hand as if he'd use the damn thing any minute. 'The problem is, I'm out of pocket, and that just won't do.' He paused. 'Will it? So, what can you give me, mate, because I sure as shit don't want the goods back now you've opened the boxes. You need to pay me before the end of the day.'

'I have nothing, I told you that. Nothing until I can sell them to someone else, and that takes time to set up. To build trust.'

'Trust!' Beefcake laughed, loud and hearty. 'That's fucking rich, that is. Come on, think. There must be something you can give me.'

'There is nothing. Just allow me to set up a sale with someone else. Give me a week.'

'A week? A fucking week? You're taking the piss, mate. No, I want payment by tonight.' Beefcake lifted the gun and waved it around.

I winced, trying to hold back a shriek.

'Or you lose a leg. Or an arm. Or maybe one of my fellas will bash in your kneecaps. Choice is yours, really. Lots of choices and all.'

Silence stretched for a while between them, taut, tangible. I studied Beefcake in the lull. He was incredibly sexy in a don't-fuck-with-me kind of way, exuding shedloads of menace and sacks full of I've-killed-without-a-second's-thought. He shouldn't be making me quiver with – with what? Need? Longing? The desire for an extreme bit of rough in my life? – but he was – even though I fancied myself in love with Liuz.

'There is one thing,' Liuz said, jerking me out of my musings. 'But you may not want it. I have no money, but I can give you a good time as payment.'

'You can fuck right off!' Beefcake said. 'I'm not that way inclined, mate.'

'No, no, you misunderstand me. I meant a woman.'

'Fuck that. Women are ten a penny.'

'This one is different, I assure you.'

Beefcake slid his gun back into his pocket and bunched his hands into fists at his sides. 'In what way?'

'She will do anything I say. Anything you want.'

Oh, God, he was talking about me, wasn't he?

'So you reckon. Bet she isn't into taking it up the ass, though. None of them are, not really. They might let you do it but they don't enjoy it.'

'This one will and she loves it, loves everything you can give her.'

'You sound a bit sure of yourself, mate.'

'I am, because I promise you, she will do anything I tell her to. She will come over and over, milking your cock with her hot little pussy until you feel like she is draining your blood through your balls.'

Beefcake was silent.

'Anything,' Liuz repeated in a thick, gritty voice. 'Anything at all.'

Oh my God, he made me sound pathetic, but he was right. I would do anything for Liuz, even fucking that man there, and what's more, I think I'd enjoy it.

Beefcake chuckled. 'All right, I'll give her a go. Bring her here to me tonight.'

'No, you come to my place. That way you know where I live in case she does not fulfil the payment, yes? I will not run from what I owe. I want to build trust with you.'

'One round with her ain't going to cut it.'

'How many do you want?'

'I'll decide that later, once I've seen whether her ass is worth fucking again. Write down your address.'

Beefcake stepped out of view, and while they were occupied, I took the chance to get out of the warehouse, my mind whirling with images of that man shoving his cock into my ass, his hands all over me while Liuz watched, maybe even joined in. Could I do that? Would I?

I knew I damn well would.

Outside, I hiked in a long breath of crisp air and ran over the wastelands, ignoring the twinge in my ankle. The urge to laugh bubbled inside me. Liuz would be emailing me today after all, and I needed to get home fast in order to reply promptly.

At the bus stop, I waited, tapping my boot on the pavement, excitement spiralling through me at tremendous speed. I was going to get a good fucking, I knew it. I'm already wet at the thought and my bottom was clenching in anticipation.

Chapter Seven

I arrived home, dashed into my office and booted up the laptop. Only then did I start stripping off my layers and examine my now-throbbing ankle. It was swollen over the inner joint and a mauve bruise was settling in the dip below. I poured a medicinal glass of wine and opened my email.

Sure enough, there was a message from Liuz. It had been sent fifteen minutes earlier.

'Hello, Aniolku, I hope you will not let me down tonight. I am very much looking forward to making a whore of you again.'

'I still have a report to write.'

I couldn't resist playing with him. I knew I would go to his flat in a few hours' time. How could I resist? But he'd dismissed me last night, kept me hanging, so now it was my turn to make him sweat a little.

'I watched myself fucking you this afternoon, and could not help jerking off again. You are so damn sexy, so fucking dirty. I love the way you sound when you come, when you hold your breath and then squeak the air out in strangled cries and yelps. Let me make you sound like that again, soon, tonight. I need to hear your pleasure echo around my room and feel your pussy milk my dick.'

Oh, he needed me all right. To pay his debts. Any normal woman would tell him to fuck right off. Why should anybody be used? Why should I be used? More to the point, why should I let some brute shove his cock up my little virginal ass in order to pay Liuz's debts? Dodgy debts, not bank manager debts, but East End gangster debts for God only knew what illegal merchandise.

Liuz didn't know where I lived. I could just block his emails. I would never have to have contact with such a depraved, moral-less man again. It would all be over in an instant.

End of.

Stop.

Of course, that wasn't going to happen. Liuz had become my everything, my whole world, and the meaning of my existence. Not to mention my warped sanity depended on going to him and being made to feel like a dirty, worthless slut again. If I didn't I'd go insane pacing my flat, masturbating, tearing at my hair, my nails.

I knew sooner or later I'd need to seriously examine where these new depraved needs had come from. Had I been repressed about sex in my teens? Was I hiding some weird degrading sexual experience deep in my memory, kind of like a blackout, but it was something I'd enjoyed even though I knew I shouldn't? Guilt was a powerful emotion, it could do strange things. Perhaps I'd been a whore in a previous existence and this was the afterlife catching up with me.

I shook my head and gulped my wine. Now was not the time to examine my own Freudian psyche or think about glitches in reincarnation. Not when getting fucked up the ass loomed before me like a warped treat. A trip to the West End it was not, but it thrilled me utterly.

The idea of a cock in my ass was not new. In fact, Liuz and I had talked about it often over the last few weeks. He'd told me he would love to take my anal virginity. Open my delicate sphincter with his fingers, ease out the tightness before slotting in his wide dick. He said he would be gentle the first time, but the first time only. Then I'd have to take it like any other dirty bitch would. Hard and fast and right to the root of his cock every time he pushed in.

'I have another two hours' work to do at least,' I told him as butterflies fluttered in my belly.

'And then come to me. You know I will make it worth your while. Now that we have met I have an even better understanding of what your horny little body needs. I have seen into your soul, Hannah, seen what filth exists there and how it needs satisfying, indulging. You know I am the only one who knows how to make you feel that way.'

Sweat pricked its way up my spine, settled around my shoulders and onto my chest. An image of myself naked and on all fours in his dingy room filled my mind. Liuz and Beefcake were there, looking at me, touching me, probing their fingers inside me front and back as they discussed what they would do to my body. Who would fuck me first, who wanted to fuck my mouth, my pussy, my ass. I would be nervous, but not about anything physical. Just about letting Liuz down. He needed me to help him with his debt. He was offering me to someone he needed to impress. Surely that made me a prized possession. My obedience, my sluttiness was something he was proud of, wanted to show off.

'I'll do my best to be at yours in two.'

And besides, even if he hadn't met with Beefcake and needed my services tonight, he'd still said this morning that he wanted to explore my slutty tendencies again this evening.

Further proof that we were meant to be together.

* * *

I dallied getting ready. Shaved my entire pussy while bending over like a contortionist in the shower, and slathered my body in a rich body butter that smelled of vanilla. OK, I was a slut, but I could still smell nice.

The bus was late. I stepped on, highly aware of my itzy-bitzy skirt riding up my thighs. An old guy with a bulbous nose ogled my legs as I moved along the aisle. He made me feel dirty and cheap, but not in a good way.

As I walked down Liuz's street I noticed that it must be refuse collection the next morning. Several sagging black bags burst from the tops of kerb-side wheelie bins, their indeterminable contents bulging and drooping over the rims. One had been pulled open, probably by a hungry, agile cat, and big white birds, gulls, fought over what looked like a half-eaten kebab.

After being buzzed in, I entered Liuz's building. Murky air embraced me. It was stronger than last night. I guessed it was the absence of any type of breeze to agitate the atmosphere. The scent settled in my nostrils, and even though it was stale, like smoke, sweaty bodies and dusty rooms, to me it was an aphrodisiac and my pussy clenched at the olfactory stimulation.

Once again, the decorated blindfold rested over the handle of number two. I reached for it with confident hands. I wouldn't be nervous, I refused to be. If Beefcake was in there waiting to bugger my ass I would be brave and stoic, learn to love it for Liuz's sake.

I rapped on the door, wondering if a camera was rolling.

'Hi, my *Aniolku.*'

I was tugged forward, and the musky, tobacco-laden scent of Liuz, which I could now identify, became intense.

'I am so glad my dirty bitch has arrived,' he said.

I could hear a note of relief in his voice and, being the double agent I was, knew why it was there.

The door slammed shut, my bag fell to the floor again, and I allowed him to scoop me into his arms. The next thing I knew, in my black world, he was kissing me, eagerly, hungrily. He probed his tongue between my teeth and set up a fast and possessive kiss.

I melted into him, my legs sinking as though standing on soft sand, my body boneless as I allowed him to support me. His kiss was so full of passion and hunger it made me feel more alive than ever before. I didn't think I would ever get enough of him.

'Ah, fuck yeah, you are all I need, so damn horny,' he said. 'Tonight you are going to enjoy being the filthy slut you so want to be.'

His breaths were hot in the shell of my ear, his words like an electric current to my clit. As he kissed around my neck and squeezed my bottom cheeks, I wondered when Beefcake would join the groping.

'Come, this way,' Liuz instructed. The relief had slipped from his voice. He was in role now. The dominant orchestrator of my fantasies was back.

I tottered forward on my heels, waiting for the pressure

in the small of my spine that would once again bend me over the table. But it didn't come. Instead, he pressed on my shoulders and urged me to my knees.

Sharp, mean carpet dug into my flesh, the sort of material that would burn if even the smallest amount of friction was generated over it.

'Suck my dick, slut, I want it good and hard before you get your ass fucked.'

Get my ass fucked. Him or Beefcake? Oh my God, this was it.

I scrabbled with my fingers, found his T-shirt-covered abdomen and then, orientated, hunted out his fly. Quickly popping the buttons, I was aware of saliva pooling in my cheeks, weeping onto my tongue. The taste of his cock was one of the most exquisite flavours I had ever known and I was desperate for it again.

'Yeah, that's it, get it out,' he said, his words abrasive and his accent thick. 'Suck me good like you did last night.'

Thick, meaty flesh filled my palm. Silk on steel and so hot it almost burned. The pulse within was fast and urgent and when I squeezed, he groaned.

My blindness slowed me for a moment, but I soon found his salty slit and licked. His fingers threaded into my stumpy haircut.

Then he was sliding into my mouth. I stretched my jaw wide, aware of my teeth scraping over his shaft.

'Ah, yes, yes, like that,' he murmured, shifting his hips forward.

My nose was buried in his pubic hair, and his glans hit my throat. I searched for his scrotum and rolled the soft sacs.

'Yes, oh yes, now suck, suck me,' he said, cupping one hand beneath my chin, stroking my stretched jawline with his thumb.

I set up small gulping motions with the back of my tongue, sucking and pulling him in. Still holding his balls, I gently dragged my nails over the wrinkled skin. Each gasp and appreciative whimper he made had moisture seeping from my pussy.

After a few minutes he pulled out. 'So good, so good, but now, now it is your turn.'

The anticipation of those few seconds was like waiting for all my birthdays and Christmases to come at once. My belly curled in excitement and my clit bobbed and swelled.

Where was Beefcake?

'Up here,' Liuz said, manoeuvering me to a standing position. 'Lie on the bed and take off your panties.'

He directed me to the bed. The crumpled material was soft on my palms and the mattress thin when I sat.

Quickly, I slipped off my underwear. The gusset was damp and warm. I began to get myself into a kneeling position, on all fours, but he stopped me.

'No, stay on your back.'

'But –'

'Shh, you must trust me. Remember how I said I would help you this first time?'

I nodded and allowed my head to rest on the bed. He was between my legs, shoving up my tight little skirt and urging my thighs apart so the air breezed over my bare, wet pussy.

'Oh, so very pretty,' he murmured.

I gasped as his tongue stroked over my labia, thick and wide. He dove the tip into every crease and fold; then began Frenching my entrance.

I reached down and slotted my hands in his dense but silky soft hair. 'Oh, Liuz, yes, yes.'

It had been so long since I'd had the pleasure of a man exploring my pussy with his tongue. How had I let that happen? It felt so damn good. He was so damn talented.

He used his fingers to explore me too, slipping and sliding in and around my entrance, tangling with his tongue as he circled my clit.

Before long an orgasm was building. A tight coil wound in my pelvis and wanted release. The sensations shimmying over my pussy were so exquisite, so intense. I could hardly tell what was tongue and what were fingers. In the blackness it didn't matter – only what he was creating inside me existed.

I curled my toes and fisted both Liuz's hair and the sheets. He slid a finger into my ass.

'Oh, oh.'

It went in easily and didn't hurt. It was just the newness of the sensation that had me writhing and gasping; sweat popping on my cleavage.

Another finger was added just as my orgasm began to bloom. This time the stretch held a pinch of pain. Good pain, pain mixed with pleasure. And all the time his tongue was merciless, thrashing at my clit. I could feel him penetrating my pussy with his other fingers. He was taking full control of me, shunting, fucking, driving me wild.

I could hardly keep still and trembled with the need to let my orgasm rock me over the edge. But instead of letting it claim me, I teetered on the brink, my body focusing on the wriggling in my ass and the stretch of my anus. It was bliss, wicked, carnal bliss, and I wanted to revel in it for as long as possible.

Suddenly the stretch became scissor-like, sharp and slicing, and I was sure then another moist finger had breached my sphincter.

'Oh, Liuz, I – I –'

He took no notice of me calling and squirming, just continued with his ministrations, creating squelching, clicking sounds as he suckled on my clit and pumped into me.

My breath hitched, and I bit back a scream. I could hold it off no longer. The first delicious wave of climax crested then pounded through me. My whole pelvis contracted wildly, gripping the fingers in my ass and pussy. Another powerful bolt of pleasure reared from my clit, spreading hot fingers of ecstasy to my rectum.

'Liuz, oh, God, please, please.' I was calling for him to stop and to continue.

He carried on, using his warm tongue to bring me down from my high by slowly licking over my silken, sopping folds.

'That was so intense,' I gasped, still acutely aware of his fingers in my ass.

'You did well,' he said. 'But there is still more for you to take.'

He turned my pliant, boneless body, looping my leg over his arm so that his fingers stayed lodged in my ass as I was moved.

Now I was on my hands and knees like I thought I would be to begin with. My shoulders were exhausted, though I didn't know why, so I dropped my forehead on my forearms.

Was Beefcake going to join in now?

'Pretty little slut's ass,' Liuz said in a soft voice as he pumped his fingers in and out of my quivering anus.

I groaned a response, lost to the new penetration and the scent of my sex and sweat and the feel of my pussy still buzzing with aftershocks. My eyes were shut behind the blindfold. It wouldn't have mattered if I hadn't been wearing one. It was too much of a struggle to keep my eyes open anyway.

'Now my cock is going in through your back door,' he said, his breath hot on my pussy and thighs.

So Liuz was going to take me first, before Beefcake, just like he'd said he wanted to.

With a sudden slide, he pulled his fingers out of my ass.

My body shook at the loss. I wanted to shout at him to shove them back in there, but I didn't. I was submissive and taking what he gave me, and in a second, I was well aware, I might not be able to take what he gave me.

He was kissing and licking the small of my back, his hands parting my ass cheeks. I whimpered in desperation for him to get to the main event; in response he slid his tongue from my tailbone to my anus.

'Liuz,' I gasped, snapping my head up at the illicit sensation.

'Shh, *Aniolku*.'

The wide head of his cock was at my dark portal now. I trembled, fear meshing with desire. A sob escaped my lips.

He wrapped his hands around my hips and his wet, lubed glans pressed harder against my throbbing sphincter. I gripped the sheets, willed myself to relax for his entry. But I couldn't, I was besieged by the edgy, sensual torment of what was coming.

'Relax,' he hissed. 'Bear down a little.'

I did as he asked and he prodded with more insistence, forcing his way forward until my muscular ring accepted the head of his dick.

A long, low wail burst from my throat and I muffled it in the bedclothes. I was so stretched, so taut around his thickness. It was both agony and bliss.

'Ah, fuck *tak*, *tak*,' he said, sinking deeper into my open ass. 'That is so perfect. You are doing so well, so well.'

He rode in then. With no barrier blocking him, he travelled deeper and deeper. Until he was buried to the root of his shaft. I was so full, so chock full of cock. I whimpered and accepted the invasion. The sting and the filling were turning to a dense pleasure that I already wanted to be accompanied by friction and movement.

'Yes, oh, please, Liuz, fuck me, fuck my ass.'

'Such a dirty slut,' he said, trailing a caressing finger down my tense spine. 'You are so perfect.'

He withdrew so just the head of his dick sat inside me. I moaned at the hollow emptiness.

'Here you are,' he said, 'this is what you want, isn't it?'

He rode in again and I called out in delight. It was exactly what I wanted. I reached down and frotted my clit, knowing that an orgasm would soon be upon me again and wanting to feel it in every part of my sex.

He set up hard, slow thrusts that catapulted me to a dark world of ecstasy. Only Liuz's rigid cock driving into my ass existed. Feeling him bottom out on each entry, his balls tickling up against my labia and the wide root of his shaft stretching my anus, was the most divine feeling I could ever have imagined.

I tightened around him. Flexing and relaxing. Flexing and relaxing. Each time he skewered me drove me nearer to climax. My fingers were busy, my clit getting ready to fly once more.

One hard, sharp slap on my rump brought me to conclusion. The sound of his palm connecting with my flesh rang through my ears. The orgasm was a fierce ride through ecstasy that had me pulsating off the bed. He pressed me down, impaled me further. I cried out, aware of him thickening inside me as he, too, came.

He shouted something in Polish. Words I didn't understand but their meaning clear. He was enjoying his release and wanted to thank the Lord above in the most unholy of ways.

On and on he rode, slowing only when my spasming body had calmed and his cock had begun to soften.

'Oh, yes, that was so good, you are a natural,' he said, kissing my perspiring shoulder blades. 'You will be so good for me, I can tell, so good.'

'Mmm,' I replied.

He withdrew, leaving my asshole tender and scorched. It was at this point I became aware that we were probably alone in the room. I was sure if Beefcake had been there he would have at least said something during that performance. I didn't know the guy, but I couldn't imagine he was the shy, retiring sort if there was some anal sex going on.

'Come and lie with me,' Liuz said, slipping off my shoes and then my skirt. 'Take off the rest of your clothes, lie with me.'

I did as he asked and he flopped on the bed next to me, scooped me against his chest and folded me into his long arms.

I was still breathing fast and glad to be rid of clothes as I was hot and sweaty. Behind my blindfold I opened my eyes, surprised for a second when I was greeted with darkness. I had been so lost in myself that I had forgotten about my lack of sight.

'Sleep,' Liuz said. 'Get some rest, you will need it for later. You are not finished with yet.'

Later, so Beefcake was still coming.

I sighed in contentment, for this was what I wanted, to stay the night with Liuz and be fucked over and over. Pockets of sleep the only thing interrupting my body's pleasure and pleasing the man I was hopelessly in love and lust with.

Spreading my fingers over the hard hairs on Liuz's chest, I listened to his heartbeat and let his heat absorb onto my cheek.

After a while his breaths slowed and deepened. The tight curl of his arm around my shoulders relaxed. My own breaths were steady and shallow, and the perspiration on my body had cooled my skin pleasantly.

I decided to risk it.

Very gently I lifted my head, angled my face to his and then, with one hand, slipped the blindfold off.

Piercing black eyes stared at me through the dim light. My heart rate rocketed.

Shit, I had been sure he was asleep.

'My, *Aniolku*, you are so predictable.'

I stared at him. Obsession had given me a photographic memory and his angled features, craggy brows and deeply ingrained stubble all imprinted effortlessly into my brain, as did the tiny semi-circular lines beneath his eyes and the little black hairs just inside his nostrils. It was a beautiful face and I had only really seen it at a distance. But I couldn't appreciate the moment for I feared he would be angry with me for removing the blindfold and send me home. Nausea welled. He might even say 'Kilimanjaro'.

But then his wide mouth tipped into a smile. He lifted his head and planted a soft kiss on the tip of my nose.

'Like what you see?' he whispered.

Relief flooded through me and my heart soared. 'Yes, yes very much.'

Chapter Eight

I continued to stare at him, waiting with bated breath for Liuz to place the blindfold back over my eyes, taking away the chance for me to really drink him in, to implant everything about his face into my mind. I wanted the image secure so I could recall it at leisure during the times we were apart. The times I fantasised about him.

The times when I touched myself.

He remained still, gaze latched onto mine, and I wondered if I'd have the courage to let him see me studying him. Part of me wanted to stay as we were, me working out what he was thinking from the way he looked at me, but it was impossible. His eyes said nothing except that he was looking into mine. Disappointment nearly took a complete and unshakeable hold on me, but I pushed it away. Nothing should spoil this … this what? Time of bonding? Dare I hope that's what this was? Another part of me wanted to boldly appraise him so he saw me doing it, so he knew that although I'd let him have his way with everything so far – discounting my following him to the warehouse; I don't think I'd ever admit to him I did that – I still had it in me to do what I wanted. I didn't think it would be in my best interest to allow him to have me totally at his mercy, even though I'd told myself in the past I would be. Somehow, with our bodies pressed together, actually seeing one another both at the same time, gave the situation a different spin.

A rule had been broken, and I was damn lucky he hadn't said the stop word.

Perhaps he was more hooked on me than I'd imagined. What if he was capable of real emotions and wasn't just using me for what he could get, for what I allowed him to do to me? What if, what if … ?

I wasn't sure how I felt about that and decided to mull it over another time. It was too scary a prospect to indulge in fantasies about us being a couple, living happily ever after. Right from the start he'd made it clear that wasn't on offer.

So why did I get the strong feeling things had changed?

He took matters out of my hands regarding my perusal of his features. His eyes shifted from mine to look at my shoulder, where he watched his hand trail down my arm, springing goose bumps on my skin. A streak of vulnerability went through me, a brief moment of utter nakedness that I felt but couldn't wholly latch on to. The full force of it was gone as quickly as it came, but the residue remained. To be blindfolded gave me a sense of safety, me not being able to see his reactions as to whether he liked what he saw, but here, now, seeing him touch me, was a whole other sensation.

A small smile dallied on his lips before he compressed them, obliterating the tiny glimpse I'd gained into his feelings. He'd looked tender just then, smitten – or was that just my high hopes? – and it made me want to reach up and stroke his cheek. Cup it to let him know I felt the same. But I didn't, too afraid that if I moved, the spell would be broken and I'd be banished to darkness once more.

So I watched him watching me, smiled myself at the tiny crinkles beside his eyes. Were they from age or laughter? I wanted to see him laugh, a real belly laugh, to giggle with me on lazy Sunday mornings.

That would never happen.

I was just being fanciful, allowing the softer side of me to come to the fore and, inwardly, I cursed myself for it. I needed to stay on the track our journey had begun on, with Liuz my master and me the willing follower. If I tried to manipulate things, who knew what would happen? I had a good idea. He'd say the stop word, and my world would be shattered. Damn, I'd become attached and shouldn't have. No, I needed to scour these new feelings away, wash any remnants down the drain, because if I didn't, it would be over faster.

Over. I never want it to be over.

Him reaching out his hand for mine, twining his fingers with mine, brought me up short. Another show of tenderness I hadn't expected, bringing my previous thoughts and hopes rushing back.

Stop it. He was just doing that to waste time between fucks. It didn't mean anything. Not a damn thing.

'You have tiny hands,' he said, gaze glued to our knot of fingers. 'So tiny.'

Shit, his words melted me into a pool of goo. I wanted to see what he saw, to see through his eyes, but his face was telling me so much more. That little smile was back, the dimple in his cheek, and his eyes had taken on a dreamy look that I would swear expressed similar thoughts to mine.

Was he feeling something for me? Something more than seeing me as a woman he could use? I couldn't hope. Just couldn't.

To stop myself falling even more madly in love with him – or more obsessed – I dragged my sights from his face and stared at our hands. I shouldn't have done that. What I saw were hands that belonged together, his large palm pressed against my smaller one, the tips of my slim fingers barely peeking from between his thick, longer digits. My stomach rolled with the realisation that I had allowed myself to go too far when I'd removed the blindfold. I'd encouraged intimacy, ousted the security blindness had given me, and I knew I was in all kinds of trouble now.

'Do you think,' he said, still studying our hands, 'you could have another man after me?'

Oh, I knew where this was going, why he'd asked that question. Beefcake. I tensed, hoping he'd think it was a natural reaction to his query and not that I knew what was going to happen at some point tonight. I swallowed, hoping my voice came out strong when I replied. Should I give the true answer burning my tongue? The one where I was honest and said that no man would ever match up to him? No man would ever make me feel as sexy, as dirty, and as needed as he did? Or should I shrug it off, behave as I was supposed to and give him a hell yeah?

I decided to hedge my bets, play it safe. 'Um, in what context?'

'It's simple. Just like I said. Could you have another man after me?'

After me. He meant tonight, me having another man straight after he'd been inside me. I could, would do that for him.

'Well,' I said, dredging courage up from the shadowy little corner it had retreated to when I'd taken the blindfold off. 'You've made it clear we're not going anywhere. You let me know we're just fuck buddies, so I haven't got attached.' Liar. 'So when you say the stop word, yes,

113

I'd fuck someone else.' Eventually. When I picked up the pieces of my heart and glued them back together.

Oh, hell. I'd really gone and fallen for him, hadn't I?

I'd said what he might want to hear, but at the same time I'd made it clear that when he said the stop word, I'd become attached to someone else. I'd effectively told him I belonged to him and him alone until he ended what we had. Those were my true thoughts, but I knew without doubt that in order for him to keep his knees intact, to have unbroken arms and legs – or worse – I'd give myself to Beefcake.

If Liuz picked up on what I'd actually said, would he send Beefcake away? He couldn't. He had no alternative but to pay the man one way or another.

If only I had the money to give him.

He sighed. 'But imagine if I did not want to say the stop word yet.'

Yet. He was going to end it at some point. Oh, God, Hannah, you stupid, stupid woman. What have you got yourself into here?

'Maybe I want to share you with someone,' he continued, stroking his thumb over my inner wrist.

'I'm not sure what you mean.' I must have sounded dense, but I needed to stall him so I could think on what he'd just said. He was putting it in a nice way, making out he wanted to share me. So he wasn't going to admit that I was payment, that I was a nothing who didn't deserve being made privy to what he'd planned. I understood why he couldn't say. I mean, how rude would that sound? You see, *Aniolku*, it's like this. I owe a dangerous man some money ... But on the other hand, he was asking my opinion. He cared enough to find out whether I could handle this instead of just assuming I would.

That had to count for something, didn't it?

Whatever it counted for, I grabbed hold of it and hugged it to me.

'What I mean is, I need to share you with someone. Maybe one time, maybe two.'

Need. He hadn't said he wanted to.

'What brought this on?' I asked, looking into his eyes. Every nerve in my body seemed to be screaming, making me tense, my mind full of questions I had no time to answer.

'I have ...' He stopped, unhooked his hand from mine and lifted his arm to cup my cheek. His eyes flicked left to right, left to right, showing me he was unsure of how to word things.

Those actions had my emotions soaring. He cared. He bloody cared!

I warded off a huge smile, saying instead, 'You have what?'

His hand burned my cheek, and his thumb tip brushing the soft skin beside my eye almost – almost – had me crying. I was on dangerous ground in more ways than one here.

'I have a problem I need your help with, *Aniolku*.'

I laughed, reverting back to my original role, of who he thought I really was. 'You need help from me? Now, that isn't the man I know. You've given me the impression you don't need help from anyone.'

'I do not usually need help, but tonight I do. Something went wrong.'

'Something went wrong?' I purposely made my voice light, acted as though I had no idea what the hell he was talking about. 'With what? And what's another man fucking me got to do with it?'

He had two options. He'd either confess or make some bullshit story up.

Please let it be a confession.

He sighed again, moved his hand from my cheek to cup the ball of my shoulder. Stroked languidly, circling my skin as though the action calmed him. Or maybe he was doing it to pacify me, to butter me up?

'I – I promised you to someone else,' he said bluntly, the words in his usual brittle, no-nonsense form but his eyes giving him away. He stared at my forehead, took his hand from my shoulder to fiddle with my tufty hair.

'You did?' I said, going for the incredulous tone.

'I did. How do you feel about that?'

'Uh, well, I don't know. When this started, it was

116

between you and me. No mention of other men or women. I thought ...' I paused for effect, hoping my acting passed as genuine. 'Anyway, why are you bothered how it makes me feel? This thing we have, it doesn't involve caring, does it? You tell me what to do and I do it. If either of us don't like it, we say the stop word.'

He tensed, stopped playing with my hair, and looked me right in the eyes. 'Will you say it now? The stop word?'

I felt a bitch for teasing him, but I wanted – needed – to know for sure if he had any proper feelings for me before I wasted my time allowing mine to grow stronger. Yes, we'd only fucked twice, but we'd spoken for a long time before that, built a rapport. Knew things about one another we'd never told anyone else. We had a bond, albeit based around a whore fantasy where we indulged in our deepest desires, but a bond all the same. Possibly tenuous, the strands of it that held us together ready to break at any moment, but it was there.

I just had to strengthen it, that was all.

'I'm not sure,' I said. 'Depends on why you need this man to fuck me.'

'I owe him money for a deal that went wrong.'

Oh my God, he'd given a full confession. Well, not full enough that I knew what he'd bought and couldn't sell, but I hadn't expected this level of admittance. Of trust.

'And you offered me as payment, is that what you're saying?'

He resumed with teasing my hair between finger and thumb, staring at what he was doing. Nodded. 'I did. I did not want to, but I did. This man needs payment. You were the only thing I could offer. Will you do it?'

I reached up and covered his hand with mine, drew it down to the space between us, holding it to my chest. 'I would do anything for you.'

Relief bled out of him, his whole body relaxing, and a gusty sigh of his sweet breath shrouded my face. 'Thank you, *Aniolku*, thank you. You have no idea how much this means to me. No one has ever –' He pressed his lips together.

'No one has ever what?' Say it, please say it.

'It does not matter.'

He touched his forehead to mine, closed his eyes, and we rested there for a while without speaking. My mind raced, my emotions a giddy swirl with me unable to distinguish the difference between them. They all melded as one big lump, settling in the pit of my stomach, a heavy stone that made me feel sick. He'd trusted me with a confidence, something I never thought he'd do. Earlier, in the warehouse, when I'd seen him offering me to Beefcake, I imagined he'd have taken his usual attitude and told me another man would be joining us and that was that. Hell, when Liuz had fucked my ass, I'd expected Beefcake to join in, striding out from behind the curtains or wherever the hell I thought he'd been.

But Liuz hadn't just assumed.

The information had me glowing.

'When will he be here?' I whispered.

'Soon.'

'Am I allowed to see him before he fucks me?'

'I think you have the right, yes. But the blindfold. I want you to wear it when he – I do not want you to see how him fucking you –'

– makes me feel? Is that what he was going to say?

'I understand,' I said, giving him a soft kiss that could be taken any number of ways. It was up to him to work out the real reason for that softness, if he even wanted to. 'How will I see him then, if I have to wear the blindfold?'

'We will watch for him through the window.'

I made to move away, to get up and go to the window. Half sitting, with my hand braced against the mattress, I was stopped by Liuz gripping my wrist and squeezing. Looking up at me with eyes that spoke of regret.

'You said what we have doesn't involve caring,' he said.

I held my breath, pulse throbbing in my neck, heart beating so hard my chest hurt. 'I did. That's what you said, what you've always implied.'

'I lied.'

Holy fuck.

'That's dangerous, Liuz.' I pulled away, making it clear he'd made a mistake in saying that. Scooting off the bed, I prayed my answer worked to my advantage. That I hadn't just made one motherfucker of a colossal mistake. For all I knew, he could be messing with my mind, trying to find out whether I'd allowed myself to feel more for him than he'd like. In order to keep him in my life for as long as possible, I had to act as I thought he expected me to.

I walked to the front window, parting the curtains a bit to peer out into the street. The mattress pinged, Liuz getting off, and his footsteps padding across the room made my tummy roll over. He was right behind me then, body pressed to my back, hands coming around to hold me close. I resisted the urge to tip my head back and rest it on his shoulder. His hot breath met my neck a second before his soft lips brushed the skin.

'I know it is dangerous, Hannah. I did not expect this.'

'Me neither!' I said on a low laugh, giving in and lifting my arms to curl my fingers over one of his forearms.

I wanted to say so much more, to turn to him, bury my face in his neck and blurt out exactly how I felt, ask him to tell me what he was thinking, but a shadowy figure emerged from the darkness at the far end of the street and became visible as a large man as it passed under the streetlight.

'I think the man you mentioned is coming,' I said.

Liuz stepped to my side and opened the curtain some more. He sighed, a shaky exhalation that made me feel sorry for him.

'Yes, that is him.'

We stood in silence as Beefcake approached, watching him climb the front steps and jab a meaty thumb onto the bell button. It was as though we were suspended, neither one of us able to speak, both wishing we had time to digest what we'd said, to understand the ramifications of his confession and the fact that I'd hidden my true feelings. Self-preservation I know, but was it fair to leave Liuz in the dark, wondering if the feelings he had for me weren't reciprocated?

I had no time to ponder on it, because Beefcake pressed the bell again, the expression on his face one of anger and impatience.

'The blindfold, Hannah,' Liuz said, voice a little rusty.

He led me back to the bed, and I sat while he covered my eyes. I could smell him, wanted to touch him, tell him everything would be all right. But I didn't. I had the upper hand here, and until I had time to myself where I could think about everything properly, I had to maintain my usual role.

'Are you ready?' He placed both hands on my head, buried his fingers in my hair.

I nodded and took in a deep breath. 'I'm doing this for you, remember that.'

'I know.'

I switched off sweeter emotions and hauled in those that belonged to the other me. The prostitute. The slut.

The dirty bitch.

Chapter Nine

The latch clicked open.

'Is she here?' Beefcake's rough voice.

'Of course.'

'Good.'

I heard footsteps, the slam of the door and the scrape of a lighter. The fuggy smell of smoke touched my nostrils.

'She looks really fucking young.' Beefcake's voice, sudden and right next to me.

His hot breath breezed onto my chest and his body heat crept over my nakedness. He wore a strong-spiced aftershave that mingled with the tobacco and my own sexy, sweaty scent. I wondered if he'd put it on for my benefit.

'She's perfectly legal,' Liuz grunted. 'And more than willing.'

'So you said.'

Someone grabbed my tits. Beefcake I presumed, for the

thumbs that squeezed against my nipples were calloused and sharp and not as refined as Liuz's.

I caught a gasp, more out of surprise than anything. In my black world I had no idea when anything was coming.

The fingers scuffed over my breasts, tweaking and pulling. My nipples hardened rapidly. I hated to admit it, but the immediate rough handling and the grittiness of Beefcake's tone had my juices gushing again. He was appraising me, like goods in a store; was I something worth investing energy in?

I let out a low moan and arched my back for more stimulation.

'Mmm, mmm,' Beefcake murmured.

A stronger hit of smoke filled my lungs, as though it had just been blown in my face.

'Horny little bitch, isn't she?' he said.

'Oh, yeah, very.'

My heart was going like the clappers and my stomach clenched. I loved the way he was groping me. It made me feel like a real possession of Liuz's.

'What's her name?' Beefcake again.

'I do not know. I just call her Dirty Bitch. She comes round whenever I tell her to and lets me screw her however I want.'

'So you've fucked her asshole?'

'Yes, of course.'

Beefcake pressed my right nipple in on itself. The sensation made me squirm.

He gave a gruff laugh. 'OK, she has potential, but first we need to discuss business.'

There was a pause.

'Oh, she will keep her mouth shut,' Liuz said. 'She won't risk not coming here any more and getting what all dirty bitches need.'

How true a statement.

Again Beefcake laughed. 'Good, but actually I have plans for her to keep her mouth open.'

He moved away and I heard one of them pull on a cigarette and blow out the smoke in a fast, tense way.

'Over here, Dirty Bitch.' Beefcake's voice.

I moved to the edge of the bed. Liuz helped me stand by wrapping his hand around my upper arm and tugging. He then guided me across the room.

My knees were weak with excitement. I had no idea what was in store for me but I had a feeling it would be deliciously degrading. When I'd seen Beefcake in the warehouse he'd been vulgar and boorish, not the kind of man I would have looked twice at in the street. Liuz's strong bony features and long, lean limbs were more my thing. But now, the thought of Beefcake doing what he pleased with me, in front of Liuz, made him just perfect.

'On your knees,' Beefcake instructed.

Liuz urged me down, but he didn't need to. I dropped willingly, and as the carpet dug into my knees, Beefcake's thighs spread around me, trapping me close against the shabby sofa.

'What have you got to drink?' Beefcake asked. 'None of my watered-down poison. I want some real stuff to sup on while she sucks me off.'

Liuz let out a stiff laugh. 'Absolutely. How about some JD. It is a new bottle.'

'Let me see.'

There was a bang of a cupboard door, the clunk of glass and then movement at my side.

'Yeah, that looks the real deal. Pour me a big one.' He stroked over my hair, tugging slightly at the blindfold. 'Now you can get my big one out, bitch.'

Heat thundered between my legs. I was going to suck his cock. Give a complete stranger a blowjob while he sat with Liuz, drinking whiskey and talking business. I was such trash, such lowlife; sucking cock was all I was good for.

Trembling with excitement, and whore sex the only thing I could think of, I reached for his dick. He'd already pulled his jeans down and all I had to do to reveal his erection was shove at his boxers.

He shifted his ass and pushed his clothing further away. A heated, raw scent drifted up to my nose. His spicy aftershave mixed with maleness and musk.

'Get on with it,' he barked when I took my time

running my fingers up and down his meaty shaft. 'I haven't come here for a fucking massage.'

Quickly, I reared up. Fisted his shaft and aimed his glans at my mouth.

'All of me, right to the back of your throat.'

I did as he asked and allowed his chunky, hot cap to slide over my tongue and palate to the very deepest part of my mouth, right to the point where my gag reflex was only a millimetre away. He tasted different to Liuz, heavier, more feral. There was a dangerous sharpness to him.

He tensed his thighs around me, squeezing my shoulders. 'Thanks, Biros, cheers.' There was a tinkle of glasses being touched then he slurped. 'Keep going, bitch, keep going until I tell you to stop. Yeah, just like that.'

As the scent of cigarettes lessened, the sofa shifted slightly.

'She is hot, yeah?' Liuz asked, his voice now coming from my right side. 'You like?'

'Yeah, it's OK for starters. But first we need to discuss some hot goods you're supposed to have shifted for me.' His voice was strained, but not so much that he didn't sound in control.

'You know I am sorry about that. But I made progress just an hour or so ago, another lead which, if sound, could have the whole pile shifted by this time next week.'

Beefcake replied but I barely listened. I was busy setting

up a bobbing and sucking rhythm. Applying hot, wet, gliding pressure along the length of him with my tongue. I licked his glans when I reached the top, dipped into his slit and tongued his frenulum.

'Ah, fuck, careful doing that.' Pressure on my head, urging me back into my original rhythm. 'You'll have me blowing in your face.'

His words, his actions, and Liuz watching me give my best performance was one of the horniest moments of my life. My pussy buzzed like it was full of electricity. If I'd thought I would get away with it, I would have frigged myself off while I rode up and down on Beefcake's dick. A few deft nudges and I would come. But I had a very strong feeling that wouldn't be allowed.

This wasn't about my pleasure.

I deepened my stroke, using my hands on the base of his shaft that my mouth couldn't quite accommodate. I gave a long, hard suck 'n'-swirl right to the tip.

'Oh, yeah, yeah, that's it, do that again,' Beefcake said, voice scratchy, breathy, like a gale over sandpaper. Control, it seemed, had gone.

'Come on her tits,' Liuz said. 'Make her yours.'

'Yeah, hold her for me, then. Get behind her and shove her tits together.'

Beefcake gripped my scalp, tugging my head up and down his shaft. My tongue was now coated in salty pre-cum and his shaft had thickened and hardened to the point that it felt un-fleshlike, more made of metal or granite. Only the slightly shifting skin at the base gave away the fact it belonged to a human.

'Ah, ah, yeah – now!' He shoved my head upwards, roughly, at the same time Liuz wrapped an arm around my waist and pulled me standing.

I blindly flailed my arms for purchase, eventually gripping Liuz's forearms as he mashed my breasts together and tipped me forward.

Beefcake grunted, groaned. The soft sound of friction filled my ears, and his panting breaths blasted onto my perspiring body.

Liuz was roaming his fingers over my taut nipples, plucking and pulling as he forced me lower, so I was bent over Beefcake, ready for him to come on.

'Oh, fuck, yes, yes. I'm gonna shoot, argh –'

Beefcake's jerking legs jostled me in Liuz's arms as warm splatters hit my chest.

'Ah, yeah,' Beefcake moaned. 'Fuck, yeah, really hot tits covered in my jizm.'

More warm cum landed on my breasts and in the hollow of my throat, immediately cooling and trickling. Liuz's breaths blew hot and hard in my ear. His bare chest pressed up against my back made me feel loved and adored. I wished he'd kiss the side of my neck. I wished he'd throw me on the floor and fuck me stupid.

I knew he wouldn't.

'Ah, yeah, she's got a good mouth,' Beefcake panted.

Liuz tugged me backwards then released me, and I sank to the carpet.

'Yeah, tell me about it.'

Beefcake grunted – it almost held humour.

'You want another drink?' Liuz asked.

'Yeah, why the fuck not? This is my night off, after all.'

I heard the sound of pouring then Liuz was back next to me.

'I'm gonna have this drink and then fuck her ass,' Beefcake said.

A tremble of anticipation besieged me. My slit was already sopping and swollen, my asshole still scorched from Liuz's invasion. The thought of Beefcake's big dick tunnelling into me was both terrifying and deliriously sexy. Also the thought of Liuz watching me get fucked was such a turn-on. What would he do? Would he play with my clit, pull my breasts? Would he sit quiet in the corner and try to ignore another man fucking my ass?

'Lie down, slut.' Beefcake's voice. 'And keep still.'

I scrabbled to do as he'd asked. The cum on my chest was drying, pulling my flesh like glue as I stretched out on the concrete-hard floor.

'I need to take a piss before I can get really hard again,' Beefcake said. 'And I think I'll do it on her.'

My whole body tensed.

No, not that.

I craved sex, orgasms, fantasies fulfilled. Not filthy piss on me. That was never on my list of to-does.

I sensed Beefcake standing, coming closer, and I shifted away. The thought of his urine arcing towards me, splashing over my body, was too foul to contemplate.

Kilimanjaro.

I should just say it and get the fuck out of here. Let Liuz deal with the consequences of his fucked-up deals and his disobedient whore.

'Ha, you don't do this to your whore often, then,' Beefcake grunted.

I pushed to sit up but his gritty boot landed on my chest and held me down. Disgust and fear raced through me.

Kilimanjaro.

But I couldn't say it. The stop word was too powerful, too final. If I said it now everything would be over between Liuz and I. That was something too huge to instigate.

When he'd first told me we had a stop word I'd felt safe, like he'd handed me a key to get out if I needed to. But now it was the opposite. The stop word was no key, it was a lock and it was keeping me pinned to the floor and about to be pissed on by a garish brute.

I braced for the splash, the revolting impact.

'No,' Liuz said, from right above me. 'No, use the bathroom.'

'Fuck that, I want to see her steaming with my hot piss.'

'No.' Liuz's voice was dangerously low. 'I am not into that.'

'Fuck off, I am.'

'I do not want your stinking piss all over my carpet, so go and use the bathroom like every other fucking visitor.'

There was a long, tense moment. Hard silence stretched between them. It could go either way. I hoped Liuz hadn't ruined it for himself. Beefcake had been told that I would do anything. That I was a shameless slut and could be used and abused and would enjoy every foul minute of it.

'Yeah, 'cause it's a really fancy carpet,' Beefcake scoffed. The pressure on my chest lifted and I wriggled to the side. 'But OK, where is it then?'

'Through that door.'

Relief washed through me as his heavy footsteps thudded away.

'Get her on the bed,' he called. 'I'll be ready to go again in a few minutes. That blow job was just for starters.'

He didn't shut the door, and as Liuz pulled me to my feet I could hear Beefcake's stream hitting the toilet water. I wanted to hug Liuz, thank him for saving me from something he'd instinctively known was not part of my slut fantasies. He knew me so well, this man of mine. Cared for me even in the face of danger.

But I didn't hug him or even speak. Instead, I allowed him to manoeuvre me onto the bed, on my hands and knees. I hung my head low, and blood rushed to my cheeks as my ass went high.

'Ah, such a sweet, slutty ass,' Liuz murmured. His hands were on me. Slippery hands slick with some kind of oil. 'Let's make sure you're well lubed.'

My jaw went limp as he drove greased fingers into my puckered hole. The filling sensation made my pussy dissolve into a whirling mass of need.

I needed to be fucked.

The horror of moments ago evaporated. Now I just wanted cock in me. Anyone's cock would do, the bigger, the harder, the better.

I was such a slut.

Liuz continued, stroking my inside walls and easing out the tension in my tight band.

'I want to come,' I whispered at the sheets.

Liuz leaned over me. I hadn't thought he'd heard me, but he obviously had. 'Come loud and hard, *Aniolku*, so that he thinks he is the best in the world at fucking ass.'

'Yes, yes,' I panted, part in response to his words and partly because of the way he was pumping his fingers in and out of my anus. The sting, the stretch, it was sublime and created a hotwire of bliss to my clit. My inner thighs were damp and hot and I could smell the hunger of my sex wafting around me.

'Get outta my way.'

Liuz slipped his fingers from me. I whimpered and twitched my hips, searching for something to penetrate me.

'Oh, she's so fucking hot for it,' Beefcake said, his words fast and tripping over themselves.

'She is, she loves it up the ass; but here, go in wearing, fuck knows where else she has been,' Liuz said. 'Dirty fucking slut.'

His words were like an aphrodisiac. Yes, I was dirty, my fantasies were filthy. Not only that, I was, along with Liuz's help, realising all the depraved, toxic acts I'd dreamed about.

'Ah, yeah, the look of that puckered little hole has got me hard enough to hammer nails,' Beefcake said admiringly.

'Yeah, I have lubed it up for you.'

A long finger drove into me, sliding in easily because of the copious amounts of lube; Liuz's, I thought.

'It is good and tight,' Liuz said. 'I have not worn it out yet, not like some sluts, their assholes get overused, there is no fun left in them.'

'Yeah, can't fucking stand that. This one looks barely breached.'

I curled my toes and fisted the sheet, recording every detail of what was being said into my memory. They were talking about me like I was a piece of meat with a hole. Nothing more than orifices for them to fuck.

It was perfect.

The digit slipped from my ass, but no sooner had I registered its absence than an impossibly wide pressure was exerted.

'Ah, yeah, here goes.'

With one jarring thrust Beefcake plundered into me.

I wailed as my whole body was thrust up the bed. But he didn't stop, he came with me, grabbing my waist and dragging me further onto my impalement. The pain was exquisite, the filling so damn acute. My anus was still sore from Liuz's entry earlier but this sting only added to the cacophony of brutally blissful sensation.

'Oh, she's like a fucking virgin in here,' Beefcake groaned. 'So fucking tight around my dick.'

He pulled almost out, then shoved back in with a heavy, slapping lunge. I braced my arms, locked my elbows, for there was nothing tender or gentle about the way Beefcake was now fucking my ass. He was going for it with gusto, incorporating all of his bulk and muscles to ram into my small body.

'Oh, oh, oh, yes,' I panted.

'You like it, don't you, whore?' Beefcake said.

'Yes, oh, your cock is so big. Fuck me, fuck me harder.'

'Dirty Bitch.' Beefcake grabbed a handful of my hair and pulled my head back. 'I'm going to come in your ass, and you're going to come too, get it? Get it, whore? I want you to come too.'

'Yes, yes,' I cried. 'Please.' I tried to reach my clit. I needed some stimulation on my blisteringly aching bud.

'Get down there, Biros,' Beefcake ground out. 'Lick her cunt so she comes with me. I can't last long in here and I want to feel her squeeze my dick as she explodes.'

I was vaguely aware of Liuz moving beneath me, his shoulders jostling my torso. I tried to let him in, but the position was too awkward.

'Fuck, no, like this.' Suddenly I was lifted up, Beefcake's cock still lodged deep in my ass as he moved us around.

I pitched my arms to the sides, disoriented as I was spun and my back hit his wide, hot chest.

'Argh, oh God,' I cried out as the angle of his dick changed in my rectum. He was sitting on the bed and I was sitting on him, his thick shaft lodged high and deep, every last inch of it.

'Oh, yeah, that's it, oh fuck, now I'm so fucking high in you. Can you feel every last inch, slut?'

'Yes, oh, yes, but –' I was hovering on the brink of climax. I just needed my clit and my pussy to have some attention.

'Now lick her, fuck her with your mouth,' Beefcake said hotly near the shell of my ear. 'But keep your attentions well away from my dick, got it?'

Liuz, thankfully, wasted no time in obeying. He shoved between my legs and slid his strong, wet tongue up my sopping folds. Began treating my desperate clit to hard, circular rubs.

I grabbed hold of his thick hair and sank my nails into his scalp. I was mindless with the need to orgasm. He was going to take me there, where I needed to go. I trusted him.

'Oh, yeah, writhe like that. Fuck yourself on me,' Beefcake groaned, mauling my breasts, pressing them flat to my chest and then bunching them together. 'You are so fucking dirty.'

Yes, yes, I was dirty, which was perfect because this filth was just the kind of thing I got off on and they were giving it to me in bucketloads.

Liuz worked my clit with even more tongue pressure. I moaned in delight, my head dizzy, as though all the blood in my body had rushed to my sex. It was swollen, pulsing, trembling, and when Liuz shoved his fingers into my pussy I could contain myself no more. I dropped my head back against Beefcake and dug my heels into the mattress. I rocked my body so I was grinding against cock and tongue, taking myself over the precipice of ecstasy.

'Oh, oh, oh, I'm coming. Oh yes, fuck me, like that.' My whole body tightened, stiffened then cascaded into a series of delirious spasms.

Beefcake let out a roar that turned into a wild groaning noise as he propelled his hips upwards. He wrapped his arms around me and twisted me onto my front. Liuz was forced to abandon his oral efforts as my face hit the mattress and Beefcake hammered out his release.

'Ah, yeah, you're loving it, loving it, fucking hell, yeah, argh–' His dick erupted and after a final lunge he flopped on top of me. 'Argh, yeah,' he groaned into my ear.

I gasped for breath. His weight was so heavy. Air had been forced from my lungs as he'd dropped down and I couldn't replace it. My pelvis was still contracting, my hips writhing, and I was savouring every last pulse of pleasure my intense orgasm had produced. But I could hardly breathe – breathing was becoming near impossible.

I squirmed and tried to push up. The blindfold added to my fear of not being able to catch enough oxygen.

'Mmmph,' I managed, pushing my arms against the bed. 'Get … off.'

'Hey, give her some air.' Liuz's voice.

Beefcake ignored him.

'Come on, you want to fuck her again, she needs a pulse.'

The weight lifted from my chest. I sucked in a much-needed breath, inflating my flattened lungs.

'Yeah, even I ain't into that,' Beefcake said breathlessly.

He pulled his cock from my ass with a small popping sensation and my tight pucker contracted. He lifted up and the bed rose as he stepped away.

I didn't move, just lay there, feeling thoroughly fucked.

'Where did I leave my drink?' Beefcake asked.

'Over there.' Liuz's voice, tight, strained.

Footsteps then silence.

My thoughts turned to Liuz. He would be pleased with me. I'd done what he'd asked. I'd been fucked up the ass to appease his debt and I had come loud and hard.

There was the bang of an empty glass on the counter.

'I'm going to save that other fuck for another night,' Beefcake said. 'Let's say tomorrow, to encourage you to sort out that shit by next week, Biros.'

'Yes, it will be gone by next week. I promise you.'

'It had better be.' There was movement towards the door. 'Because I know where you live now.'

Chapter Ten

With my ass pleasantly stinging from the previous night's much-wanted abuse, I stood behind the large tree in Liuz's street. I performed yet another mental list check: beanie hat and sunglasses on; food in my backpack; camera around my neck for quick access; voice recorder in my back jeans pocket.

It had taken me a while to fall asleep once I'd returned home last night. After going through the events of the evening and dissecting everything, I'd then concentrated on what had been said. Beefcake had mentioned alcohol, 'none of my watered-down poison', and I assumed that was his business – hooky liquor. It was a problem I'd touched on before in a story, people selling alcohol they'd bought in Europe, diluting it and attaching freshly sealed caps and British labels. If Beefcake turned out to be a pain in the ass – in a different way – I was sure Trading Standards would welcome my anonymous telephone call.

But that might get Liuz in shit.

I didn't want that, but who knew what could happen in the future? Liuz might hurt me more than I was prepared to take, so I filed that plan in the back of my mind in case I needed it later.

It was always good to have a plan or two.

It had rained overnight, and the earthy smell of wet mud lingered in the air. The grass verge beneath my feet was spongy, and I was mindful of my footing. I didn't fancy spraining my ankle again anytime soon. Today I had to be alert, not allow myself to become distracted by the beauty of Liuz when he appeared. And he would. He'd written to me earlier, thanking me for letting Beefcake use me as he had, and told me he'd be heading out today to try and clean up the mess he'd found himself in so I wouldn't have to do it again. I gathered he meant selling the alcohol, visiting the buyer he'd mentioned to Beefcake last night, possibly trying to get the purchaser to hand over the cash faster than they'd originally agreed.

Did that mean Liuz cared enough about me that he didn't want Beefcake having access to me whenever he wanted until Liuz had come good on their deal? Or was it a purely selfish, jealousy thing on Liuz's part – that he didn't like sharing me? I hoped it was both, because the warm and fuzzy emotions those thoughts inspired made me feel loved and wanted. Special. Worth something to someone. Despite the somewhat sordid bent on everything, it was always good to feel loved.

I stared at Liuz's window to take my mind off what I'd already analysed in bed last night. I could only go over things so much before they became blurred or a tangled mass of questions I couldn't answer. I needed a clear head today.

His curtains were closed, still with the slight gap in the middle where we'd peeked out at Beefcake. Every time I thought of that episode it came back with startling clarity, as though it was happening all over again. It had been branded into my mind as new experiences usually are, and I hoped the images wouldn't fade with time. They were one set I'd prefer to keep vivid forever.

It wouldn't be long before Liuz came out. It was nearing noon, the time his emails went silent every day. Right on cue, the main front door opened and he emerged from the building, looking divine in light-blue jeans that hugged his muscled thighs and a black bomber-style leather jacket with woolen ribbed cuffs and hem. The fleeting wonder of how that wool would feel if I rubbed it came to mind, and a surge of moisture flooded my sex, my stomach rolling over in my excitement. How did such a small thing set me off? Or was it just him and everything about him that brought on such a reaction? I didn't have time to give it much consideration, because he closed the front door and jogged onto the path, walking towards my hiding place with determined strides. Hands in his pockets, head bent low, he strode past me, thick-soled black boots beating the pavement. His scent followed in his wake, and I sniffed long and deep. Another flood, another stomach roll.

God, that man had the ability to send me to my knees.

I ought to be careful of that, of letting him have control like this. But what was I supposed to do? It seemed my body had a mind of its own, and no amount of telling myself to take a step back and not get so attached wasn't going to work. He had me, hook, line, and bloody sinker.

Stepping out from behind the tree, minus twisting my ankle, thank God, I followed him like I had before. He didn't head for the warehouses this time but came to a halt at a bus stop around the corner. Great. How the hell was I supposed to get on the bus after him without being seen? To wait in the queue without him sensing me there? And I was sure he'd sense me if I got up close. How could he not? We were so in tune with one another.

I was still a fair few paces behind him, but good old fate was on my side again. A double-decker bus trundled up to the stop, and Liuz disappeared inside. I watched him through the windshield. He paid the fare and took the staircase. I ran to board while he couldn't see out of any windows.

Once on the bus, I plastered on my best smile and stared at the driver. He was a rum-looking, dark-haired man who needed a good razor and an undisturbed night's sleep if the stubble on his jawline and dark shadows under his eyes were anything to go by.

I realised I had no idea where this bus was going.

The driver stared back, eyeing me as if I had air inside my skull instead of a brain. He sighed. 'Where to?'

Shit. 'Um, a round trip. Fancy a bus trip. Nice bus trip. Yep, a good old journey on a bus. Can't beat it.' I closed my mouth before I bleated anything else and made a complete fool of myself.

He frowned, his chest inflating with another sigh – a weary one, I'd bet my last quid on it – and jabbed a few buttons on his ticket machine. Paper streamed out – far too much for a bus ticket in my opinion – and I ripped it off. Glancing at the cost, I swung my backpack off my shoulder and ferreted about for my purse. Another sigh from the driver. I hadn't expected a bus ride, hadn't thought to have my purse closer to hand, and the driver's hot stare on the top of my head as I bent it wasn't the most comfortable of experiences. Of course, my purse decided to play games and remain hidden. I had a moment's panic where I wondered if I'd even remembered to pack the bloody thing. Just when I felt the need to bolt off the bus and abandon this insane mission, the purse slid into my hand. I pulled it out, paid, and scuttled the hell away from the driver.

I sat at the back on the relatively empty lower deck, occupied by an elderly lady with a red-and-black tartan shopping bag tucked between her Hush-Puppied feet and a male youth, unwashed for a couple of days if I was any judge, iPod in hand, bobbing his head to whatever music youths listened to these days. I squished myself into the corner and slouched so the headrest of the seat in front kept me hidden. Feeling safe that I'd covered everything, I settled down as the bus heaved away from the kerb. Where were we going? I slipped my purse into an outer compartment of my backpack, zipped it securely, then studied the ticket again. It didn't tell me much, just a series of acronyms that could mean our destination was anywhere.

The bus stopped and started so many times to let people on and off that I stifled the urge to scream. I felt tense at not knowing where we were going, the bus only touring the streets of Brixton; but in a way I should be pleased we weren't going anywhere more further afield. At least I was fairly close to home and could get back quickly if things turned pear-shaped.

And what if they did? What if Liuz was meeting another man like Beefcake, one who had a penchant for handing out right hooks that resulted in broken noses, among other things? I shuddered at the thought. It was all very well me getting involved with Liuz, my own little bit of rough; but with other bits of rough on the scene, what had started out as my need for a sex rush could turn into something rather nasty. No one knew where I was going today – and really, they wouldn't want to know about my latest escapades anyway – but if something went wrong, no one would be able to find me for days. Or ever.

I had to stop thinking like that. These men were dangerous, yes, but come on, did I really think they were high-ranking gangster types who could have me disappear without a trace?

Unfortunately, yes, I did. I knew enough from snooping for my job to spot a dodgy man when I saw one, and Liuz and Beefcake were dodgy. I liked to think Liuz was less so. I couldn't imagine him knee-capping someone, resorting to terrible violence to get what he wanted; but then again, I didn't really know him, did I? He'd only shown me the side of himself he wanted me to see, a knife with a sharp edge that could cut if mishandled but was perfectly OK to play with so long as I was careful and just held the handle.

The bus bell buzzed, a mechanical, wasp-like sound that sent my heart pounding. Footsteps clattered above then on the staircase. My stomach muscles contracted, the thought of seeing Liuz appear sending me lower into my seat. I peeked through the space between the two headrests in front, the fuzzy fabric scratchy on cheeks growing hot from the subterfuge. My nerves, God, they seemed to rattle and ping all over the place, and if I wasn't careful I'd be sick. I didn't usually feel this way when working, but this wasn't the same as work. This was mixing business with pleasure.

Liuz came into view and walked straight from the stairwell to the double doors ahead. They opened with a wheeze and a whine, and I shot out of my seat and trotted down the aisle. He stepped off into an empty street filled with abandoned houses, their windows boarded up with steel rectangles. Wonderful, a dodgy setting to go with the dodgy men. No one but myself and Liuz were about, so if he turned to look behind himself he'd clock me right away. As the bus pulled away, I darted into a hedgerow bordering a front garden, twigs grasping at my hat and sending my sunglasses askew. I parted the leaves and watched Liuz. He didn't go anywhere, just stood at the bus stop as though awaiting another bus. And maybe he was, but gut instinct told me he'd been instructed to wait there. He looked around, eyes keen, hands no longer in his pockets. Did he need them free in case trouble found him?

As though he'd heard my thoughts, he fisted his hands. Crap.

A screech sounded, like an angry bird ousted from its nest by a usurper, and I jumped a little, holding in the shout of surprise that sat on my tongue. At one of the houses opposite, a man stood in the doorway, a big brutish bastard who didn't look like he was a stranger to illegal boxing matches. Liuz walked across the deserted street and came to a stop in front of the beast, who was a head taller than my man and about a foot wider. Liuz nodded, and they went inside, leaving the door ajar.

It was fate, wasn't it? How could it not be when so much seemed to go my way? Normally, that door would have been shut up tight and I'd have to find some other means of eavesdropping. But, like the warehouse episode, the way had been left clear.

I scrabbled out of the hedge, a small fight between me and the twigs ensuing, then ran across the street, not worried about being seen due to the steel over the windows. I crept up the short, broken-concrete path leading to the front door. The garden hadn't been tended to in God knew how long, the grass knee-height and coarse, any flowers in previously cared-for borders a thing of the past. I positioned myself against the side wall of the house to the right of the front door and strained to listen.

No sounds came from within, and curiosity got the better of me. I sucked in a long breath and decided to go inside. It wouldn't hurt if I stood in the hallway. I pushed the door open a little more and listened again. Still no sounds. Stepping inside, I waited in the small foyer, spying a battered old shoe lying at the bottom of the stairs that a previous tenant must have left behind.

Or did the shoe belong to someone the man had dealt with?

Before my mind ran away with itself, I cut off those

kinds of thoughts and took a couple of steps forward to stand beside what I assumed was a living room doorway to my left. A doorway without a door. I looked into the shadows ahead and saw nothing but a dense grey mass. No darker body shapes interrupted it, so I assumed Liuz and the man had either gone further into the house or upstairs.

Upstairs it was. A floorboard groaned above, and I went to the bottom of the stairs and gazed up into more greyness, brighter than it was in the living room because of the front door letting in light. Quietly, I climbed six carpeted steps, praying none of them creaked. They didn't. I pulled the recorder out of my pocket, held it between two baluster rails, clicked it on, and waited.

I didn't have to wait long.

'So you will do it?' Liuz asked.

'I will.'

If the only other man in this place was the one I'd seen at the front door, his voice was just as menacing as his appearance.

'The trouble is,' the man said, London accent as thick as Beefcake's, 'he has people who'll know you had this sorted. People who know he's dealing with you. He might not tell them how he's extracting payment off you, but they'll be well aware to look in your direction if something happens to him.'

'I have thought of that. I want you to do it while I am with him.'

'You fucking what?'

'I want you to come to my flat while he is there. Make it seem like a break-in gone wrong.'

'Right.'

Were they discussing what I thought they were discussing? Was Liuz asking this man to hurt Beefcake? I wasn't sure if I wanted to keep my voice recorder on.

'So,' the man said after a long pause. 'What happens after I've done and gone?'

'I will call the police. Report it. News will get back to his men that way.'

'Yeah, he'll have coppers in his pocket, no doubt about that.'

'And I will have a witness.'

'Nah, that's just getting messy, mate. The less people involved the better.'

'She will not know anything except what she sees.'

Oh my fucking God...

'She will give the police a statement that corroborates the fact someone burst into my flat and killed him.'

I held in a whimper of shock.

'Killed him?' the man asked. 'That's a bit steep for what's going on between you, mate. I thought you meant roughing him up a bit, know what I mean? If anyone has a grudge against him, one that excuses killing him, it's me. For what he did to my –'

'Rough him up, then,' Liuz said. 'But enough for him

149

to know he must not mess with me, at the same time making it look as though it has nothing to do with me.'

'That's a tough one. How'd you expect to get your point across while keeping your nose clean at the same time?'

'I will tell him people are after me, that it is best he does not visit my flat again. I do not want him near my witness after this. She is … I do not wish to pay him in the manner he wants to be paid.'

'Let me get this straight. You owe him money and you can't pay him until the end of next week when you sell whatever shit it is for him that you were supposed to sell before. In the meantime, he's getting payment from you some other way – I don't want to know how. So if you can't pay him, how the fuck do you expect to pay me?'

'I have enough to pay you. I have it here. With me.'

'What, you've got enough on you to cover the cost of killing him? That's what you originally wanted, yeah?'

'No, what I have on me would have covered a retainer for that. Or at least a payment to show good faith.'

'Right. So you're telling me you've got two grand on you, yeah?'

'I do.'

'Show me.'

The shuffle of papers seemed to scream out.

'Fair enough,' the man said. 'How come you couldn't give him this two grand?'

'He wants all the payment in one go.'

'How much do you owe him, for fuck's sake?'

'Ten.'

'Shit. Rather you than me, mate.'

'So you will do it? Break in and hurt him?'

'Yes.'

'When?'

'Tonight.'

With my heart hammering, I slunk down the stairs and out into the street, switching off my recorder and putting it in my pocket. I glanced up and down the street, refusing to entertain thoughts of the coming evening. I didn't need to ask myself if I would be Liuz's witness. I didn't need to question whether I was insane – I knew I was well on the way there. And I didn't need to question why it was imperative I get back home as fast as I could so I was there to wait for Liuz's email that was certain to arrive.

An invitation to witness Beefcake being beaten.

It was wrong, it went against all my beliefs, but it seemed that when it came to Liuz, I was lost to whatever he wanted.

I jogged down the street, out of sight of the house, and waited at a bus stop. A bus would be along any minute, one that would take me close to my place. Home. I had to get home. To boot-up my computer. To sit and wait for the tinkle that told me email had arrived. And to think on what the hell Beefcake had done to that burly man that warranted him being killed.

Chapter Eleven

The shower water rained hard and heavy on my scalp, soaking my hair and streaming down my face and body. I reached for my vanilla and lotus flower shower gel and lathered up, inhaling the sweetly exotic fragrance as it infused the steamy air.

Soon I would be on my way to Liuz's again. I shouldn't be, not really. I should be calling the police or the authorities or something. Reporting the crime that was about to be committed.

'Come and be my slut again,' he'd said in his email. 'I promise it will be the best night ever.'

'How can I refuse?' I'd replied. 'See you at nine?'

'Perfect, Aniolku, perfect.'

It had been a brief exchange, simply arranging for my body, with my orifices, to come to his home. Or so Liuz thought. Because I knew better, and for the first time since our sordid affair had started I felt dirty. Dirty and hesitant. Maybe even used.

Would it stop me going?

Hell no. Liuz needed me – so what if he used me, so what if I was to be his witness? When you loved someone it was possible to do anything for them, even stand by and watch a man get beaten – or worse.

I re-lathered my body and turned up the heat on the cooling water. Another minute and the shower would turn cold then I would have no choice but to get out and put on my slut clothes.

* * *

By nine o'clock the sun had dipped below the rooftops and Woodstone Road was strewn with shadow, darkening the small, mainly paved front gardens and creating pockets of blackness between the street-parked cars.

I pushed through the front door of Liuz's building feeling almost like one of the residents. I was becoming quite a regular visitor in my miniscule red skirt and spray-on vest tops. Briefly, it crossed my mind what the neighbours thought of my comings and goings. Did they think I was a real whore? A slut who came round to be used and abused and paid with money not orgasms? The thought would have normally thrilled me, but tonight was different. Tonight I wasn't just a body, with tight wet holes crying out to be fucked, I was also a pair of eyes, a witness – an accessory.

Clacking across the foyer, I noticed, with surprise, that there was no blindfold on the door handle.

What did that mean? Had he just forgotten? No, silly me, I needed my eyes to be a witness.

I knocked on the door, but needn't have bothered because it swung open as I was tapping.

'Dirty Bitch,' Liuz said, reaching for my wrist and tugging me briskly inside. 'You are late.' The door slammed. Liuz didn't flick the latch.

His face was tense; his craggy brows hung low and his cheeks looked a little sunken. He shoved a hand through his hair, and it flopped back messily around his forehead, one strand just touching the long lashes around his left eye.

I wasn't late. It was nine on the dot.

'About time.' Beefcake's gritty, deep voice came from where he sat on the sofa.

My heart stuttered and my stomach clenched. He was here already. There was no time for me and Liuz to talk or fuck – it was straight down to business.

'You remember Grant from last night?' Liuz asked, pressing his hand into the small of my back and urging me forward.

I swallowed, mouth dry, and stared at Beefcake, or rather, Grant, as he turned his big meaty face and leered at me. Suddenly I felt grateful for the blindfold last night. His lumpy, bald skull shone disconcertingly, and his fat, squashed nose was shiny and red. Small black eyes narrowed further as he scanned me up and down. What had first been a sexy, don't-fuck-with-me allure was now so infused with menace that I would have quite happily turned and walked away.

Except I couldn't. Liuz needed me.

'Not the oil painting you hoped for, eh?' Beefcake said, standing. 'Just goes to prove you don't need a pretty face to be able to fuck well.' He knocked back the remnants of the amber liquid in his glass and set it aside. 'And fuck you well I did. You were screaming for more.' He walked over to me and cupped my chin. Whiskey-laden breath washed over my face. 'Well, you're going to get more. I'm going to fuck your tight little ass again, over and over until you're raw and bleeding and begging for me to stop making you come.' He slid his hand from my chin, down my throat and to my breast. He squeezed, hard, uncomfortably.

I barely suppressed a whimper.

'What's the matter, Dirty Bitch? You not up for it tonight?' His attention snapped to Liuz, a frown furrowing his fleshy brow.

'She is always up for it,' Liuz said, spinning me to face him and forcing Beefcake to release my breast.

The urgency in Liuz's gaze harnessed my attention; he darted the tip of his tongue out and swept it over his top lip. Then he kissed me, deeply and passionately, filling me up with his flavour and his strength. I clung to him, fisting my hands on his soft, black T-shirt.

He was communicating with his mouth. We didn't need words. We were so connected, so in harmony with one another. It was clear he was telling me to be strong, to re-find my slut-self and give a good performance. He needed me to do this. He needed his Dirty Bitch to be by his side during this dangerous time.

I would be there for him.

Heat pooled in my pussy as he roamed his hands over my back, my ass cheeks and up my skirt. Parting my legs to give him better access to the gusset of my thong, I allowed myself to melt into him, delighting in the feel of his body against mine. He delved his long, elegant fingers into my wetness, and a gasp escaped as he probed high, with two, maybe three fingers. I clenched around him, a gush of creamy moisture leaking from me.

He broke the kiss and withdrew his fingers.

I opened my eyes and staggered slightly as he released me and stepped away.

He held up his hand. 'See this,' he said. 'So fucking wet for it, she is dripping. It is always the same, cannot ever get enough cock.' He put his shiny index and middle finger into his mouth and sucked noisily, closing his eyes and giving a low, approving growl.

The sight had me near to combusting. I didn't need to search hard for my slutty-self, she had seared back into the room like a bolt of lightning. Every cell in my body screamed fuck. I needed filling with hard, hot cock, and the sooner and the faster the better.

Beefcake huffed and glanced at my flushed face and parted lips. 'Yeah, I see your point.' He shucked out of his jacket and placed it on the back of the sofa. The way he laid it left a shiny black handle visible.

Gun.

Fear turned my stomach as a whole host of blood-red images peppered my mind's eye. Death. Severed body parts. Smoking barrels. Arteries pumping their liquid contents onto the ceiling, the walls, the carpet.

My knees turned watery, my spine soft.

Liuz put his arm back around me. He flicked his gaze from the gun to my face. 'I've got you,' he murmured into my ear. His voice dropped lower, like a warm breeze over meadow grass. I could almost have imagined it. 'Play the game.'

'What's the matter with her?' Beefcake grunted, shoving down his black, grimy jeans to reveal Homer Simpson boxer briefs.

'Nothing,' Liuz said. 'She is fine.'

'Maybe we should blindfold her again.'

'Nah, she is good.' He gave me a little squeeze as if to jolt me from my daze.

'I, er, I like your boxers,' I managed.

Beefcake gave a snarl, which balled his cheeks and

showed teeth that were surprisingly good. I guessed it was as close to smiling as he ever got. 'Yeah, from my kid last Christmas.'

'Oh … nice.' He had a kid. Shit, I really didn't want to be part of murder that would leave a child fatherless.

But it wouldn't be murder. Just a rough-up.

'Like I said earlier, Biros,' Beefcake said, 'I'm going to fuck your slut every night until you pay me and tonight I'll fuck her ass and you can fuck her pussy.' He stepped out of the colourful boxers and tugged at his thick shaft. 'But no fucking funny business, keep your hands where I can see them.' He stabbed a nail-bitten finger at Liuz's chest.

'Hey, I got no fucking desire to touch your dick,' Liuz said, shoving Beefcake's arm aside and screwing up his nose. 'Believe me.'

'Yeah, well, make sure you don't. Come on, bitch, get on there and strip. I want to see you naked and writhing under me.'

Oh my God. They were both going to fuck me at the same time.

Moving to stand by the bed, anus and pussy quivering, I was aware of Liuz close behind me. When I turned to face him, his top was off, showing his lovely wide chest and his stacked abs. His scent embraced me, smoky and raw, hot with desire, dense with confidence, but there was something else lacing it too. It was hard to pinpoint.

Fear perhaps. No, maybe impatience, apprehension. The kind of sweat-laced smell men going into battle emitted.

When was the violence going to happen?

One side of Liuz's mouth tilted, and his dark gaze bored into mine. Without a word he peeled my top over my head, his movements tense, deliberate.

If only I could comfort him, assure him of my support. But how could I when for the second time in our relationship I'd followed him, spied on him? I pushed down a flutter of nerves. He needed me to be strong for him. Play my part in the scene he'd orchestrated.

Like the puppet I was, I let him release my bra and drop it down my arms. He tugged at my skirt and thong, and I rested my hand on his concrete shoulders as I lifted first my left then my right foot, allowing him to slip the garments over my feet.

Finally, with steady, dexterous fingers, he undid the straps on my heels and removed them.

'Fuck, come on, get on with it,' Beefcake grunted. 'You get inside her first, Biros, and then I'll shove in. Fill her up.' He strode over to us, rubbing his hand up and down his cock. The head was such a deep beetroot colour it was almost purple, and his big, hairy balls swung as he moved.

Liuz's face hardened as he crawled onto the creased covers of the bed, pushing down his jeans and underwear as he went. He didn't remove them completely; just let them

159

bunch at his thighs. 'Come ride me, slut,' he said, his eyes flashing and his cock bobbing. 'We're going to fuck you so good tonight. Two big cocks inside you. What do you think of that? Isn't that what you have always dreamed of?'

I cleared my throat, smoothed my hands over my breasts and tweaked my nipples. 'Yes, it's what I've dreamed of.' I had to get in character, not think of Beefcake's kid or the big burly bastard who could arrive any second.

Liuz pulled at his cock, stroked his finger over the slit, then made a circle with his index finger and thumb around his shaft. He pumped hard but slow, making the veins bulge and the head swell further. 'You want me to fuck you, don't you?'

Nodding, I crawled eagerly onto the bed.

Yes, I wanted Liuz to fuck me. Yes. Yes.

But did I want Beefcake again too? What if Liuz had ruined me for everyone else? What if only he would do now, forever, for the rest of my life?

'Good, dirty slut,' he said in a soft voice as he rolled a condom on. 'That's it, climb on board.'

I set my knees either side of his hips and hovered my entrance over his cock. He held it dead upright; a glorious solid shaft for me to impale myself on.

'Ah, yes, come on,' he said tightly as I took him that first inch.

I tipped forward, flattened my hands on the pillow his head rested on. He hissed in a breath as I took more of his cock into my dripping pussy. There was a bead of sweat on his forehead, and he flared his nostrils. The coarse hair on his chest abraded my nipples.

He glanced at the door.

Panting out a breath, I palmed his cheek and brought his gaze to mine again. He would give the damn game away staring at the door.

But as he turned back to me there was something different about him. In the depths of his eyes I saw a man who needed to be loved, a man who craved affection and companionship. Suddenly I realised a truth.

Liuz was lonely.

Well, not any more, now he had me. Forever.

As if to prove my thoughts, for words were not necessary, I braced and took him right into my body, as deep as he could go, in one hard plunge.

'Ah, yeah, fuck, that's it,' he said, screwing his eyes shut. 'Now move.'

In a second.

That first bite of pain as my pussy stretched to accommodate him, that first filling, was euphoric. It released endorphins on a grand scale. I wanted to savour the moment.

His eyes shot open. 'I said move, Dirty Bitch, get on with it.'

I cried out as a sharp sting razored into my ass. Liuz had slapped me, and not a playful tap, a really hard whack that rang around the room.

But it was OK. He'd done that before. I knew just how to let the pain bloom across my flesh and sink into my clit. It was good pain, pain that melted to bliss.

'Ah, oh yes, yes,' I cried, setting up a grinding motion with my hips. 'Oh, yes, fuck me, slap me, fuck me.'

He paddled me again with his palm, three times more. Each slap had him increasing the thrusts of his hips. Each heated rise of pain swelled my clit and dampened my pussy more. I was here for my lover. I would do whatever he needed me to. Loyalty and passion sent my heart rate rocketing and my body coiling up like a big spring, storing up urgent sensations ready to be blasted out.

The bed dipped.

'Oh, yeah, so red, that's it,' Beefcake said, hands on my hips, blocking Liuz from slapping me again. 'I love a red ass. Get ready for it, bitch, we're going to make you burst.'

'You wearing?' Liuz grunted.

''Course I fucking am, you think I want her germs?'

My clit was bashing against Liuz's wiry pubic hair, the sensation exquisite. I slowed my wild thrusting and let the pressure build. 'Ah, Liuz,' I gasped onto his lips.

'Hold off,' he whispered through gritted teeth. 'Hold off.' He gripped my upper arms, supporting my feeble, lust-ridden body. 'Please.'

Beefcake was busy, rubbing my hole with his fingers, spreading my copious natural lube around the taut wrinkles of skin.

Liuz glanced towards the door again then sank his teeth into his bottom lip.

Whatever he was expecting to happen – I wanted it to wait. Beefcake had wriggled a finger into my anus and was rotating it, as if drawing circles. Easing out the tension and stretching me. I groaned as desire surged through me and bucked my hips back for more.

'Ah, yeah, filthy whore, here you go, is this what you want?' Beefcake removed his fingers, and in one brutal surge shoved his cock into my ass.

'Argh!' Searing pain sliced through my anus. He was so damn big and hard and I was already so full of Liuz's cock.

Liuz grabbed my face, pulled my mouth to his, and kissed me long and deep, capturing my subsequent cries in his throat.

'I love this tight ring,' Beefcake ground out. 'Fucking brilliant.'

He withdrew, plundered back in.

My whole body trembled. Lights flashed behind my eyelids. My clit was still harnessing pressure, my pussy, stretched and full, was swelling and weeping. And my back chamber, although on fire, was bringing to life all the memories of being fucked the day before. I was getting ready to let it all explode.

Orgasm. I needed to come.

I tore open my eyelids. Liuz's deep stare, only two

inches away, greeted me. His eyes were narrowed. A small muscle ticked below his left socket, fast, over and over. He glanced at the door yet again.

'Oh, yeah, oh yeah,' Beefcake shouted, ramming into me, faster and harder. 'Oh fucking yeah.'

The backs of his thighs whacked up against my ass each time he sank deep, and his balls slapped into my swollen labia. They must have been hitting the base of Liuz's shaft, or even his balls. But Beefcake, despite his homophobic comments earlier, seemed beyond caring.

So was I. My orgasm was within reach. 'I'm going to … I'm going to … ah yes, yes.'

There was nothing I could do. I had reached that precipice of perfection. That sublime state where it just feels so damn good and every nerve in my body, every cell, was as full of pleasure as possible. And hovering there, in that exquisite state of existence, with my pussy and my ass so full, was divine. It was as if everything in my life had been leading to this one physical sensation and this one act of love for Liuz.

Suddenly it was over, release took hold, and I became a writhing, spasming mass of orgasmic waste. I cried out. The sensation of pulsing and throbbing around so much solid cock, while I was so stuffed, was a hard, wild, almost painful ride. Sweat popped over my body, my sex gushed and my anus contracted, squeezing the base of Beefcake's dick like a noose.

'Ah, yeah, that's it. Good girl, ah, ah,' Beefcake said.

He dug his fingers into my hips so bitterly I knew there'd be rows of bruises. The speed of his thrusts increased and his noisy, rasping breaths buffeted down onto my back. He was close, so close.

A thunderous bang forced my eyes open.

After that everything happened so quickly, it was hard to keep up with events.

Liuz shoved out from under me. Beefcake withdrew and pushed me to the floor in his scrabble to get off the bed.

'Who the fuck are you?' Liuz's voice; loud, angry.

I scrambled into a kneeling position, used the bed as a barrier between me, the angry men and the masked intruder who had burst into the room.

'What the fuck?' Beefcake bellowed, lunging for his jacket, his rock-hard cock flicking up against his belly and his ass wobbling.

Liuz tugged up his jeans and marched up to the imposter who stood, feet apart, just inside the doorway. 'Get out of here,' Liuz demanded, fist clenched, back muscles tense.

The interloper, the brawny, tall guy from the abandoned house earlier – I recognised his jacket – darted his gaze around the room, as if surprised by the scene that had greeted him when he'd flung open the door.

In that split second, Beefcake grabbed his gun and pointed it at him.

Chapter Twelve

Insane as it may be, given the situation and all, I couldn't help but look down at Beefcake's groin again to see if he'd lost his erection yet – or pulled up his pants. He hadn't on either count. Did fear also turn him on? God, he was one hard bastard – fear on a stick. I glanced from his dick back up to his gun hand. It didn't shake, which was more than could be said for me. Yes, I'd known this was going to happen, but actually facing it was another thing altogether. My heart beat so fast it hurt, and adrenaline scoured every bit of me.

Masked Man pulled out a gun of his own, pushing Liuz backwards then closing the door. Liuz ended up beside the bed, well out of the way of the action. And that's when real fear overtook me. I glanced at Liuz, who widened his eyes at the way things had turned out, everything so out of control compared to the easy rough-up they'd planned. Who knew Beefcake would be carrying? Who knew Masked Man would be too? This wasn't how it was meant to be.

I screamed, thinking that was what would be expected of me had I not known about this mad scheme, and thankfully diverted Beefcake's attention. He looked from Masked Man to me, his frown so deep it twisted the skin of his fat forehead.

'Shut that fucking bitch up!' he snarled.

Masked Man took the opportunity to step forward and kick Beefcake where it would hurt most, and I winced, expecting him to crumple onto the floor writhing in pain. He didn't. Was this guy used to pain in that area? Did he participate in sex games I'd only heard about? Why was I even thinking thoughts like that anyway? It was like my brain was directing me to think about anything other than what was actually happening; the enormity of it and what could potentially occur.

'Please,' I said, clutching my hands together over my chest. 'Take my bag. I have money in there. Credit cards. I'll give you the PINs. An iPhone. You can sell it, make a bit more cash.'

There, that had sounded genuine, hadn't it? After all, if this was supposed to be a break-in gone wrong, wouldn't I have assumed he'd busted in to make off with whatever he could get his hands on?

Beefcake and Masked Man ignored me, staring one another out like some crazy duel was about to take place. Beefcake's face was flushed – the only indication his cock and bollocks were undoubtedly screaming in pain right now – and he tightened his grip on the gun, pulling back the trigger.

'No shooting!' Liuz shouted, holding his hands up. 'Please, do what she says. Take her bag.'

Ordinarily I'd have been offended by that. Take my bag? The cheek of it! But I'd get it back later anyway, providing Masked Man returned it. 'Yes, take it. Please, just go.'

Masked Man and Beefcake continued to stare, so I risked another peek at Liuz. He, too, was flushed, and lowered his fists to his sides.

'Who are you? What do you want?' Liuz asked.

Masked Man blinked slowly, as though Liuz's question bored him. 'Doesn't matter who I am,' he said, his voice gravelly, very different to the one I'd heard earlier. 'This doesn't concern you and the woman.'

'Oh, so this is about me, is it?' Beefcake said, his cock finally deflating to a semi-erect pose. 'Come on then, out with it. What the fuck is this all about?'

'You know,' Masked Man said, his tone ominous and full of meaning.

Oh, he was good at this.

'No, I don't fucking know, otherwise I wouldn't have asked, would I, you stupid cunt.' Beefcake glared, eyes hard, his finger so tight on that trigger.

Didn't this man feel any fear at all? I sensed none of it coming off him – or Masked Man for that matter.

Liuz and I appeared to be the only ones who saw danger lurking up ahead. One slip of either finger on those triggers and we'd be propelled into something I really didn't want to be involved in – a witness in a story I'd so far only ever written about from an outsider's perspective. And what if Liuz got hurt? What would I do without him?

That spurred me to try to be the peacemaker, the one who sorted this whole mess out and made Liuz grateful I'd been there. 'Listen, please. If this is something between you two, please, just go. Do this somewhere else.'

'Think I'm going to let this slimy bastard get away now I've finally cornered him?' Masked Man asked. 'Think I'm going to let him get away with all the shit he's done to me over the years?'

God, this guy was brilliant.

'And what the fuck have I done to you over the years?' Beefcake took a step forward.

My stomach bunched. I needed the toilet. The two men stood about four feet apart now, and if one of them took a shot, the injury from such close range would make one hell of a blood splatter. I shook off my thoughts, annoyed with myself for worrying about the mess rather than ending this thing or keeping quiet so I could file the information away.

Beefcake rolled his shoulders. 'I don't even recognise your voice, you prick, and if I don't know what I'm supposed to have done, how the fuck can we sort this out?' He paused, for effect I guessed. 'And you know when word of this gets out, my men will hunt you down, find you, torture you – maybe for a few days, maybe not – then give you a nice new pair of concrete shoes and introduce you to my old mate, the Thames. All that, even if I'm dead.'

He sounded so menacing, and I believed him. Beefcake's reach was clearly long and wide. What the hell was Liuz doing getting involved with him? Did he need money so badly, being hooked up in a dodgy business deal with Beefcake far outweighed any consequences?

I was in deep – with this mess and with Liuz – but I wasn't going to desert my man now. When the chips were down, that was when your boyfriend needed you most. You didn't just walk away at the first sign of trouble. Still, I kept quiet, giving Liuz a sideways glance to check how he was doing. He wasn't about to get involved, standing out of the way like that, and I didn't blame him. So long as he stayed where he was, I had a feeling he'd be safe.

'You think that bothers me?' Masked Man asked, levelling his gun a bit more. If he pulled the trigger, he'd blow the back of Beefcake's head off. 'You took everything from me. I've got nothing left. So being dead would be a blessing. But I'll see you dead before I hit that fucking water.'

Beefcake cocked his head a tiny bit. Something about

that action freaked me the hell out. It was as though he didn't care he faced death.

Maybe he didn't.

'Take a shot,' Beefcake said, looking ridiculous with his pants down. 'Come on, take a fucking shot.'

Masked Man nodded, as if to himself, and squinted, finger tightening.

The door burst open, shoving into Masked Man. He went sprawling and landed on the floor, scrabbling to try and stand again. The new guest at our fright party looked a lot like Beefcake, except he was taller and had the strong air about him that he never took no for an answer. He slammed the door before kicking Masked Man under his chin, snapping his head and torso back. Masked Man growled, recovered quickly and pushed himself backwards using his free hand on the floor, raising the one holding the gun and pointing it at Beefcake.

He wasn't quick enough, though. Beefcake Number Two lunged forward, smacking the gun out of his hand and stomping his thick-soled boot onto Masked Man's chest.

'Don't fucking move,' Number Two said.

'That's it. Hold him steady.' Beefcake strolled over, hiking his pants up along the way. He zipped then buttoned up and loomed over Masked Man.

This had gone completely wrong. I quickly shifted my gaze to Liuz. He didn't know what to do, I could see that, and I didn't either. It wasn't my call. This wasn't on the original agenda. I pleaded with my eyes for him to give me a signal on what to do, but he wouldn't look at me, his gaze riveted on the other three men. I turned away to see what Liuz was seeing, and had to hold back a whimper.

Beefcake had kneeled beside Masked Man, and his gun was about an inch from our intruder's forehead – right between the eyes.

Oh, shit. Oh my God. What the hell were we going to do now?

I had no choice but to watch. If I made a run for it, I might get shot.

'You took your time,' Beefcake said, voice casual.

'Didn't know who this geezer was, did I?' Number Two said. 'Could have been some bloke visiting.'

'What, in a fucking mask?' Beefcake snarled.

Number Two shrugged. 'Well, yeah.'

He said that as though people wearing balaclavas were all the rage. And maybe they were in his world. Normal attire for people in their line of business, nothing weird going on here, please look away folks.

'You want me to do the honours?' Number Two asked.

'No, this bastard's mine,' Beefcake said. 'I haven't got my hands dirty in a long time. Reckon I'll forget how to shoot before long. A refresher will do nicely.'

Oh, no. Beefcake was going to kill Liuz's friend.

I felt sick and flattened one hand to my chest. 'Oh, God. Please, just stop this. Let me go home. Let me and Liuz go. This is nothing to do with us.'

Beefcake trained his gaze on me. 'Listen, love, you might be a nice fuck, but your voice is getting on my damn nerves. Shut the fuck up, all right? You can scream again later, once this bollocks is sorted out, know what I mean?'

He expected me to fuck him after this?

'Violence always gets me horny.' Beefcake smiled, looked me up and down, then turned his attention back to Masked Man. 'Now then. Let's see who the fuck you are.'

He yanked off the balaclava and tossed it aside. Frowned. 'Teddy?'

Teddy? Beefcake knew him?

'I do not want this in my place,' Liuz said, stepping from beside the bed to stand behind Beefcake.

'Listen, mate.' Beefcake looked over his shoulder. 'Your place, my place, doesn't matter where – he's greeting his maker. What does matter is that if we do this here, now, your debt's clear, know what I'm saying?'

I widened my eyes, the implications sinking deep into my marrow. Liuz had one hell of a dilemma. He'd be free of Beefcake if he allowed this scenario to go on – but would he really? Liuz would have something on Beefcake, but he'd be a liability, and who knew, one day it might be Liuz on his back with Beefcake's gun pointed at his face. But could my man let his friend, his associate, be shot in cold blood? The poor man had only taken on a simple job for Liuz, and the shit had really hit the fan.

I stared down at Teddy, now unmasked and, oddly, not looking frightened at all. What was it about these gangster types? Didn't they get scared about anything?

'Now, Teddy,' Beefcake said. 'I reckon it's time for you to let me in on what's bothering you. What did I do to you?'

'You know,' Teddy said. 'What you did to my Marlene.'

'But she got in the way. It couldn't be helped. If she'd have just stayed upstairs like she'd been asked, she wouldn't be six feet under, would she?' He shrugged. 'Not my fault I thought she was someone else. You remember, Teddy? She had to stay upstairs while we hid the goods.' He laughed, eyes drifting upwards as he recalled a memory. 'Those were the days, when we were just starting out. Stashing pot and a bit of coke in your sideboard. Jesus. Look how far I've come.'

The pride in Beefcake's voice sickened me. No remorse whatsoever for poor Marlene. The fact that these two had known one another for a long time shocked me, as did the way Teddy hadn't told Liuz about his relationship with Beefcake being an issue when he'd agreed to rough him up. He'd had his own reasons for doing this.

Two quick *pffts* of sound broke the silence. Beefcake reeled backwards, and Number Two crashed to the floor.

What the fuck was going on? Liuz yelled and jumped back, away from Beefcake, and stared from one fallen man to the other. I did the same, screaming, fright flinging me to the headboard. I clutched it for comfort, but nothing was going to make me feel better for a long time to come.

Beefcake had a single bullet hole in his forehead, brain and grey matter littering the floor behind him and on Liuz. Blood pooled beneath Beefcake's head, and he stared at the ceiling, sightless, his teeth bared. Number Two hadn't fared much better. A hole graced his temple and, sprawled the way he was, he resembled every dead body I'd seen on TV, minus the surrounding white chalk line. The right side of his face and head were missing.

I fought my gag reflex, fought the urge to scream long and loud, and clamped one hand over my mouth. I stared, incredulous, as Teddy got to his feet, brushed himself down, and bent to retrieve his gun.

'Now that's sorted,' he said, looking at Liuz, 'I'm off.'

'What?' Liuz said, his features pinched, his mouth opening and closing.

'I said, I'm off.' Teddy smiled. 'Just give me and my mate out there ten minutes, will you? Then call the police. By the time they get their asses round here, we'll be long gone. Oh, and tell them exactly what happened, minus the bits about me and Marlene. No names mentioned, got it?'

175

Even though he wasn't talking to me, I said, 'Got it.' I just wanted him out of here. Wanted this whole nightmare to be over.

Liuz nodded, one of thanks, I thought, and stepped aside to allow Teddy access to the door.

'You got this one on me,' Teddy said. 'Well, rather than the full fee, since I had an old score to settle anyway.' He laughed and opened the door, gloved hand lingering on the handle. 'Fuck, I forgot that.' He nodded at his balaclava.

Liuz picked it up and handed it to him.

Teddy nodded his thanks and walked out, closing the door quietly behind him.

I stared at Liuz, seeing the dead men in my peripheral vision, and shuddered. We were in this thing together, no doubt about it, bound by a terrible ordeal that I wouldn't forget in a hurry. What if the police found out we'd held information back? What if we got into trouble?

'Are you OK, Hannah?'

My bottom lip trembled. A wave of tiredness took over the adrenaline, and I slumped against the pillows. My whole body shuddered, and I was unable to process exactly what had happened. I glanced over at the window, saw the spider web of cracked glass showing between the partially opened curtains. The bullets had entered that way, then.

Liuz stepped over Beefcake and climbed on the bed,

taking me in his arms and holding me tight. He stroked my back, and I rested my cheek against his chest, trying not to think about the transference of Beefcake's blood from him to me. His heart thundered, and he shook a little. A sob built up inside me, but I wouldn't cry. Not yet. Not until this whole thing was over.

With his chin on top of my head, he said, 'I am sorry. Fuck, I am sorry. About everything, that he had to touch you again and – it wasn't – this wasn't–'

'I know. What are we going to do?'

'I do not know. We must call the police. Get our stories straight before they arrive. It is important we say the same thing. They will speak to us separately, I think. Please, I ask only this last thing of you. Please do not break down. When this is over, if you want to say the stop word, I will understand.'

Did I? All along I'd said it wouldn't be me saying that word; that Liuz would have to be the one to end our association. But now? I recalled how I'd felt not five minutes ago at the thought of Liuz getting shot and me losing him.

I couldn't.

Even if it meant spending time in prison if the police found holes in our statements?

That was a tough question. One I wasn't prepared to answer just yet.

We spent those agonisingly long ten minutes in one

another's arms. Liuz sang to me, some Polish tune I didn't understand, but the melody soothed me, and with my eyes closed I could almost imagine two dead men weren't sprawled out on his floor. If it wasn't for the metallic scent of blood, heavy on the air now, I could have pretended everything in our world was wonderful.

'It is time,' he said on a sigh.

My stomach muscles cramped again. 'I know.'

'We must go through this quickly, our stories.'

'Yes.'

'It will be all right, *Aniolku*, I promise.'

I wished his promise could be kept, but I wasn't naïve enough to believe it could be. It would never be all right. Not now. I'd have nightmares, I was sure of it, and I worried that our relationship would deteriorate with the recent turn of events. Could we get through this? Could we hold on to this terrible secret forever?

I knew I could.

But what about Liuz?

Chapter Thirteen

It was very hot at the police station – hot and stuffy and oppressive. As though they'd organised it that way so everyone felt on edge, unable to relax and would offer up their information, their truth, quickly just to get out of the place.

As Liuz had predicted, we were separated the minute the police arrived at the murder scene. I was offered a trip to the hospital for a check over, but declined, stating that I was physically fine, just shaken up with the horror at the events of what I'd thought would be a quiet evening with my boyfriend and his mate.

As if Beefcake could ever fall under the heading of 'mate'?

Stepping into my silent flat, I leaned my back against the bolted door. My stomach growled with hunger, but nausea had moved in like an unwelcome squatter in my belly – I knew I wouldn't eat for some time.

My palms were clammy and itchy, my eyes dry and my

tongue stuck to the roof of my mouth. I felt horrid but I was all right. I hadn't been arrested, just questioned, and I'd done what Liuz had asked of me. Said all the right things about how events unfolded and acted dumb when Officer Lederman quizzed me about the identity of the other victim and the murderers.

Somewhere within myself I'd also found the dignity to hold my chin up when asked about the scene the intruder had met when he'd barged into Liuz's apartment. I wasn't proud to say that I'd been in bed with two men, naked and being screwed senseless. But I needn't have worried. The declaration didn't even widen Officer Lederman's eyes. I guessed he'd seen it all before – it was just a damn shame he reminded me so much of my dad.

I wandered not into the kitchen but into my study, peeled off my clothes, right down to my underwear, and stared at my mural of Liuz.

Twice the sequence of events had been gone over by Lederman. Notes were taken while a tape recorder whirred. He'd given me a cup of tea too. I hadn't drunk it. My words throughout the questioning had been carefully chosen, though I didn't bother to hide my underlying distress at seeing two men murdered. That had been gruesome and would linger for a very long time in my memory.

But I surprised myself with my calculating mind and the strength I'd found within. I'd given up so much for Liuz, done so many reprehensible things – what did a few more matter? I won't deny I was frightened, especially when I had to scurry my mind back to things I'd said earlier, when I'd still been shaking with shock. But I remained resolute and in control. When you had everything to lose it was amazing how you found the strength to protect what was yours.

I snapped shut my curtains and flicked on the local radio. Wondered if there would be news of the Woodstone Road shooting and the murder of one of the district's most notorious criminals – I didn't know if that was the case, if Beefcake was one of the district's most notorious criminals, but my journalist mind couldn't help but pre-guess the story slant.

I bent for my box of paints and my head was suddenly filled with an image of Beefcake lying with his brains blasted out. I stumbled and dropped to my knees. Scrabbled for my palette. The shock of the image was sickeningly detailed and it jumped uninvited into my mind's eye a nasty surprise.

There was only one thing for it.

I had to get the image down despite still having Beefcake's dried blood on me. It would give me control and allow me to look at it only when I wanted to. I couldn't cope with such macabre and sudden intrusions into my own mind.

Diligently, I blobbed out the colours needed to paint Beefcake's final form. The police had asked me about him. I'd said, as agreed with Liuz beforehand, that he was a friend of my boyfriend's who'd popped around for a drink and some fun. Three times Officer Lederman had gone back to the relationship between Liuz and Beefcake. Three times I'd given the same answer. Vague and loose and playing dumb, it allowed Liuz to say what he needed without being tripped up by information I gave.

I mixed grey with blue and a little white, for it was the brain matter that was the overwhelming image of Beefcake. Then just above the skirting board, about a metre away from Liuz's painted feet, I began my gruesome picture. It was cathartic, though, and instantly I felt the release, the cleansing process of putting the image into a form that I had control over.

I wondered where Liuz was, if he was still at the station. Officer Lederman said, as I'd been released, that he was being kept for a few more questions. I hoped he was holding up all right and prayed that he was sticking to the story he'd so carefully mapped out for me and that I'd followed to the letter.

What I wouldn't do right now to be with him, hold him, comfort him. He needed me, I could sense it. It was like we had some kind of telepathy going on. He was upset and having a rough time. His woman at his side would be a good thing. I could prop him up with some of my inner strength.

Finishing Beefcake's shocked features and messy brains,

I glanced at the life-size drawing of Liuz. His brooding face, huge erection and long limbs had me buzzing, despite the horrors of the night. I remembered the awesome orgasm I'd had, riding him hard and having another cock in my ass. I'd been off-the-scale ecstatic – I'd actually feared for my sanity throughout the whole fuck. My mind had spun into another dimension entirely.

A better, sweeter image bombarded me. One that must have been reality for Teddy as he'd burst into the bedsit. It was me on top of Liuz, my head thrown back in climax, Beefcake shunting into me, his bulk vast compared to mine and his wobbly skin red and blotchy with exertion. His meaty fingers latched onto my hips.

I got busy with my paintbrush again; I was merely a puppet painting the pictures that flooded my mind. In the top right-hand corner of the wall I drew a crude bed – dank, green sheets and a shadowy brown streak for the floor. Liuz was my next addition, sumptuous orange mixed with a little brown and yellow for his flesh, the perfect sun-baked look. I tipped his head back into the pillow, his Adam's apple jutting like on the very first picture I'd seen of him. I tangled my own painted limbs over his middle, bent-up knees hiding his hips, arms reaching onto the bed, supporting myself. I'd spent years working on my craft of committing images to paper, canvas, or in this case a wall, and tonight I was glad that the act of doing it came naturally and with such an

183

easy flow. Worrying about the length of a back and the direction of light just wouldn't have helped when I had a mind full of worries about Liuz.

Would his crime of setting up a beating that had turned into grisly murders stay a secret? Of course, once more than one person knew something it technically was no longer a secret. But I didn't count, I was in love with him, nothing would ever make me tell. Plus, Liuz didn't even know I knew about his involvement with Teddy. As far as he was concerned I just thought Beefcake had finally met his match and it was damn bad luck it was at Liuz's place.

I drew Beefcake now, on his knees behind me, his hips pressed into my ass cheeks. I gave him an expression of rapture, mouth almost tilted in a smile as he looked down at where he entered me. It was his last moment of pleasure before he died. I had given him that.

Weird, but that gave me a feeling of pride.

And what about me? Would my crime stay undetected? I'd known what was going to happen hours before it had. I didn't know the name of the law I'd broken but I was sure there was one. It must be illegal not to tell the police about a rough-up that was going down.

I stepped back and admired my third image, me being fucked by Liuz and Beefcake. It was lewd and dramatic; all three of our expressions blissful and stuck like that for eternity.

What punishment would I be subjected to if I was found out? Would it be a jail sentence or a ticking off? I had no idea. There was only one thing I really knew for sure and that was I had to be with Liuz. My whole body was aching with the need to feel him against me, in me, around me. I could almost smell his skin; smoky maleness that held such a wealth of shockingly sexy memories and seductive promises.

Swiftly, I drew his hands and wrists on another spare patch of wall. Sinewy tendons and round joints covered in a fuzz of dark hair. Elegant fingers with short, square nails. I adored his hands. I needed them on me so much it hurt.

I wanted his painted hands to come to life. So I stared at them, willed them with my eyes and my thoughts. If I could have one wish it would be that he was here now, holding me, making everything all right in my world.

The doorbell jumped to life with a trill.

I started then stared into my hallway at the front door as though I could penetrate it with my gaze.

Who the hell was calling on me at two in the morning? Liuz?

I dropped my brush, dashed out of the room and tugged the door shut. Raced to the peephole. A glut of apprehension and hope poured into my soul as I splayed my palms against the cool wood and peered through.

It was him.

Elation bolted through me and my heart soared. A new wave of nausea crashed in my stomach, sending bile shooting up my gullet.

How did he know where I lived?

Perhaps I should be cautious and not answer the door. I'd never told him my address, had been very careful not to. It gave me an element of control, more power almost than the stop word.

But the bare bones of my desperation were all that existed, and I flung open the door and stared up at him.

'Hannah,' he said, glancing over his shoulder.

I noticed a blob of dried blood on his cheek.

'Can I come in?'

'Yeah, sure.'

Liuz in my flat. Oh dear Lord above.

'What's the matter?' I asked, flicking my gaze towards the stairwell.

'It is fine,' he said, stepping over the threshold. 'I got a lift here, just checking that he was gone.'

'Oh, who by, I mean, who gave you a lift?'

'A policeman. I was not allowed back to my place, it is cordoned off. Seemed sensible to say I would come and stay with my girlfriend.'

Girlfriend.

'I know,' he said, placing his hands on my shoulders and looking down into my face. 'It felt a bit odd that I did not know where my girl lived, but luckily the policemen did, and they drove me straight here without even asking me the address. Thank fuck it was you who answered this door, this was the first one I tried.'

'Yeah, I can't imagine the other three residents in this building would have been very pleased to see you in the dead of the night.'

I swallowed tightly at the choice of the word 'dead' on tonight of all nights.

He didn't seem to notice. Instead, he slid his gaze down my body. 'What you got all over you?'

'Paint.'

He pulled his brows low.

'I like to paint, it helps when I have something on my mind.'

'Can I see what you have painted?'

Oh, fuck!

'No, I, er, I haven't finished it yet. Let's, let's get a drink.' I went to move away from him, to go into the kitchen, but he tightened his hold on me and lowered his head. The next thing I knew he was giving me such a tender, soul-aching kiss that my heart melted. He allowed his soft lips to play with mine, peeked his tongue into my mouth. I drank up his flavour. It was all I would ever need, and I kissed him back with fervour, to show him that I was there for him. I was standing by him and would for all of time.

Eventually he pulled away. 'Yeah, let's get that drink. Something strong.'

I headed into the kitchen and felt his gaze on my ass. I was still wearing just my underwear.

'You hot or something?' he asked.

'Yes, it was boiling in the police station. I couldn't stand it.' I reached for two fat-bottomed wine glasses and twisted off the screw cap on a bottle of Shiraz.

After pouring two generous glasses, I handed him one and sipped on my own.

He gulped his down, more than half in one go, deep glugging sounds coming from his throat. Good wine was clearly wasted on Liuz; he couldn't have tasted even a hint of the ripe-berry flavour the label boasted.

After he'd swallowed he looked into my eyes. 'Did you stick to our story?'

'Of course.'

'You didn't mention any names?'

'No, only Beef – I mean Grant. But I didn't know his surname was Hunter, they told me that.'

Liuz nodded and tugged at his bottom lip with his teeth. I wanted to do that, I wanted to tug his bottom lip with my teeth then kiss and kiss until morning.

'How about you? Did you stick to it?'

'Yeah, it was straightforward enough. Just told them that we were having a good time.' He gave a small micro-expression, a slight wrinkle of his nose and a gritting of his teeth. 'And that we had let Grant join us.'

I supped on my wine and thought of the picture I'd

just created on the opposite side of the wall to where Liuz stood now. I couldn't let him see it. He would hate the image if just mentioning our threesome made him grimace involuntarily. Shame it was so damn horny for me, though. While Liuz had been struggling with sharing me with his enemy, I was having a wonderful time. What a fucked-up situation.

'Hannah,' he said.

'Mmm, what sorry, what did you say?'

'I said, you didn't mention any of the stuff you had heard about hooky booze, did you?' He frowned at me, like a stern parent.

I gawped at him and shoved my hand on my hip. 'No, of course not. What do you take me for?'

He gave a sharp shrug and pinched the bridge of his nose between his thumb and forefinger. When he moved his hand two white fingerprints stayed. 'Hard to know who to trust sometimes.'

'You can trust me, you can always trust me.' I set my wine aside and reached for him. Wound my arms around his slim waist and tilted my head. When I spoke again my voice was soft and soothing. 'I'm here for you, Liuz. You can count on me to be at your side, forever.'

Chapter Fourteen

He looked at me, relieved I'd say, going by the tight lines around his mouth disappearing, the frown vanishing. I'd done that, made his fears go away, and I felt inordinately proud of myself. We had something going, didn't we? Hard to deny it when we were so in tune with so many things – we were destined to meet, I'd swear it. I supposed he did have to ask those questions about him trusting me, whether I'd put my foot in it and got him into trouble – and if I had, it wouldn't have been intentionally. God, no. I wanted this man in my life for a good while to come – like I'd told him, forever – and I'd do anything to keep him there. I'd proven that with covering up a murder, for God's sake. I didn't think you could get any more loyal than that.

As I continued to sip my wine in the comfortable silence that settled over the kitchen, I pondered on exactly what I'd done. It was all very well me telling him he could trust me, but although I'd love to say I did, could I fully trust him? There would always be that little whisper of doubt, no matter how long we stayed together, wouldn't there? I knew enough about human nature to know that when backed into a corner, hurt and broken-hearted, a person might well renege on a promise and spill the God-awful can of worms they'd been storing in their mental larder. We'd done a terrible thing, knowingly luring a man to his death – and another was killed in the process, but I wasn't taking the blame for that! Who was to say years down the line, if things went wrong between us, that Liuz wouldn't use this night against me? If, later on, at the trial, say, he went up on the stand and told them all I'd been lying. I bit my lip, then realised if he implicated me, he implicated himself.

I just couldn't see him doing it. Couldn't see him saying something that would land him in prison. Yes, he was a thug of sorts, no doubt about it, but an outright criminal?

I almost laughed, because hell, he *was* an outright criminal.

Come to think of it, so was I.

I had to stop thinking like that. It would be OK so long as we were together.

'Can I trust you, Liuz?' I blurted.

I had to make sure, didn't I? I had to see the look on his face, see his eyes when he answered. I stared at him as he lifted his head, swinging his gaze from the floor where he'd undoubtedly been seeing things that had happened in his bedsit. God, I knew all about how that felt. Since getting back from the police station, despite me painting out what I'd seen to make it go away, I still saw events as they had occurred in all their sickening glory. How long would that last? And I had yet to shower, to sleep. Would nightmares come, haunting me in my sleep as well as me being tormented by my thoughts during the day? Would time fade the images, making them less sharp? Would it erase the guilt bit by bit? If I convinced myself enough times that it had happened exactly as we'd told the police, would I eventually believe it?

Again, Beefcake being shot flashed through my mind. I clenched my teeth. Gulped some wine. Fiddled with a lock of my hair.

Who would have thought brain matter would spread so far?

I shuddered and shoved the image away.

'Yes, you can trust me,' he said.

How long had I been thinking? Had it taken him a while to answer me? If it had, why? He seemed sincere, scared for a second, as though my question meant I didn't really trust him. He lifted one hand and cupped my cheek, thumbing my cheekbone and looking at me but through me. I wasn't sure I liked that, but maybe he was seeing into the future. Maybe he was having one of those daydreams where you imagine yourself with the person you love and you hope that the couple on the beach, the couple in bed making love, the couple with two kids and a puppy will really happen for you.

Did I want that? I couldn't say I wanted the whole package right now. I was too full of just wanting Liuz all to myself, let alone sharing him. Yet I had shared him.

'We'll have to give evidence in court if Teddy gets caught.' I took another large gulp of wine, suddenly too aware of what might loiter in our future. I hadn't meant to say that. I wanted to forget it all, but it seemed my brain wasn't into keeping my thoughts inside.

What if the solicitors tripped us up? What if they caught us out in our lies and we ended up being the ones taken down to the cells? I couldn't think about it any more – it frightened me to death. I wouldn't be forced apart from Liuz – not if I could help it.

'But he will not get caught, Hannah. He has gone. I do not think he will be back.'

Liuz dropped his hand from my face and paced my small kitchen, rasping his palm over his stubbled chin, his eyes darting left to right.

Now we'd started talking about it properly, I couldn't stop. 'OK, so let's say Teddy's gone to Brazil or something, right? That he's gone there because it's the safest place to be when you've had a hand in murdering people. So I've heard, anyway. Yes, let's say that. So, we need to deal with what's left. Retaliation from Beefcake's gang.'

He stopped pacing and stared at me. 'Beefcake?'

'I mean Grant. What about that?'

'What about it? I imagine they will send someone around to my place once the police have released it back to me. His men will ask questions, I know that, I am prepared for it. I will tell them what we told the police. No one except us, Teddy, and whoever killed Grant and his thug know any different. It will be all right, *Aniolku*. We cannot keep worrying over this. If we do, we will make mistakes, bring attention to ourselves. We must act naturally.'

He resumed pacing, and despite what he'd said, that alone told me he wasn't hindering his own words. Something played on his mind – a double murder and God knew what else – and I was at a loss as to how to make it all go away.

I didn't think sex was going to work somehow.

'My editor may want me to write a story about this,' I said, silently cursing my over-active mouth. Why couldn't I just shut the hell up?

Liuz sighed. 'Then do it. Stick to the story. It is an ideal way to get our version out there. Grant's people will see it. Telephone or email your office later when you have had a little sleep. Offer the story yourself. It is better that they print it before I return home. Before his men call round.'

I wondered how long I'd get Liuz to myself, here, in my flat. I knew it sometimes took weeks for the police to release a crime scene. I imagined Liuz's place, forensic officers crawling all over it, blood spatter analysts working out how fast the bullets were travelling. They'd know exactly where the shooter had been standing by the time they were finished. The alarming thought of witnesses streamed through my mind, and I tamped down the urge to voice my fears.

Still, one question was burning to be asked, and I wouldn't be able to rest until I knew the answer – or at least had my fears quieted. 'What if some do-gooder saw the killer and gave the police information that leads them to working out who did it? I mean, it only takes the smallest bit of DNA to catch people these days.'

Liuz stood still and turned steely eyes on me. 'Hannah, do you not think I have thought the same? That our stories might be straight but someone else may come along and fuck it up? I can only hope Teddy thought of that before he came to my place. That the killer is a professional who would have covered all angles. These people who murder for a living are not stupid. We have to hope we are safe.' He took a sip of wine then raised a hand to his mouth, biting on the pad of his thumb.

'Don't do that,' I said.

'Do what?'

He frowned at me as though I was getting on his nerves, and perhaps I was. I was getting on my own nerves.

'Biting your thumb, your skin. The police look at things like that. Same as reporters do. They'd have noticed your skin wasn't ripped or whatever when they interviewed you, and if they call you in again and see you've been gnawing your fingers off, they'll think the worst.' I was gabbling, I knew that, but I couldn't seem to stop myself.

'Would they not think I had chewed my fingers because I was traumatised at seeing two people killed?' His cheeks flared red and he clenched his jaw.

'I suppose.'

'You are inventing worries, Hannah. I cannot cope here if you are going to keep going over this. It will drive us crazy.'

Not stay here? He had to stay here, with me.

He paused to finish his wine, placed the glass on the side then asked, 'Where will I sleep?'

'In my room, if you want. I can join you, or if you don't want that –'

'I do want that. I do not want to sleep alone. While I am here, let's sleep together.'

A part of me melted at that. He needed human comfort as much as I did. OK, my kind of comfort was talking things through, and I guessed his was being close to me instead. If I could just learn to keep my mouth shut, we'd be fine and he'd stay.

I watched him walk out of my kitchen and followed, intending to show him into my bedroom. Before I could stop him walking into the room with the mural, he'd opened the door and had one foot over the threshold.

'That's not my bedroom!' I said, a little louder than I'd intended, but it had the desired effect.

Liuz stood still, hand on the doorknob, looking at me with his head cocked. 'I am sorry. Which room is it?'

'The next one along. That room –' I nodded at the open doorway, my heart beating way too fast '– is where I do my art. I'm shy about it. Don't like anyone seeing my stuff when I'm halfway through a project. So, um, if you wouldn't mind not going in there?'

He nodded and stepped back, closing the door. 'Of course.'

'You know I'm trusting you not to go in there at all, right?'

I'd have to get someone in to fit a lock.

'Yes, but do you not want me to get to know you a little better, though? Seeing what you have created will show me a different side to you, and you know how much I enjoy all of your different sides.'

What was he saying? That he wanted more than just fucking between us? I decided to test how much he really cared for me.

'I'm not ready to show anyone my art yet, not even you. I'm self-conscious about it.' Here goes. 'If you go in there without my consent, I'll have to say the stop word because … because you'll have broken my trust. I can't have a relationship without it, Liuz.'

What if he said it himself now? What if me thinking

I was clever in calling his bluff backfired on me? Shit.

'I understand. You saying that has made me feel better. I think – I know – I can trust you now.'

'And you didn't before?' I was hurt, I could admit that, but hadn't I had the same thoughts – that I couldn't fully trust him?

'Yes, I did, but I wondered … if later down the line …'

I didn't want to discuss later down the line. That scenario needed to remain firmly in my head. Talking about it out loud might make things go wrong, and I couldn't have that. We'd come through so much in such a short space of time. We didn't need some silly conversation to mess it all up now.

'Come on,' I said, linking my arm through his. 'Let's go to bed. We're both tired. It's been one hell of a day.' I nearly laughed again at how hellish it had been, how me saying that, like we'd had nothing more to deal with than a tiring day at work, was so ridiculous.

I led him to my bedroom, wondering how he'd look and feel in my bed, with its puffy comforter and soft sheets – a far cry from Liuz's sparse coverings. To be here now, together in my flat, was something I'd wanted – both of us sharing our spaces with the other, sharing parts of our lives. OK, it had taken two men being killed to get it, but –

Shut up.

I let go of his arm and walked to the side of the bed, pulling back the quilt and patting the mattress on the side

I wanted him to sleep. I unhooked my bra, dropping it to the floor, and eased down my panties, kicking them away once they reached my ankles. I knew he watched me, so I stretched lazily, pointing my fingertips to the ceiling. I wanted him to see what he could have every night if he only reached out and took it – took the next step, took our relationship to a higher level. If he stayed.

Suddenly I spotted my hands, covered in paint and God only knew what else. A whiff of my sex-sweat odour rose to my nose. I seriously needed a shower, there was no way I was going to spend my first night with Liuz in this state. 'Give me two minutes,' I said, gesturing to the bedroom door. 'I'm going to take a quick shower.'

'Go ahead,' he said, standing still and staring at my dressing table covered in lotions and potions and jewellery.

After dashing into the bathroom, I yanked on the faucet, doused myself in soapy bubbles, rinsed and dried, then sped back to the bedroom feeling much fresher and hugely relieved that he was still where I had left him.

'Do you mind if I shower too?' he asked.

'Sure, go ahead.'

He nodded curtly, as though snapping out of some fug, and took off his clothes. I enjoyed seeing every piece of material leave his body, comfortable to take every one of his movements in as though we did this every night of the week. It was a great feeling, me hoping that our future held more nights like this. And it would, wouldn't it? How could it not now? And if anything threatened that I would have to resort to more extreme methods of making him stay.

He abandoned his clothes on the floor and left the room.

I lay listening to the irregular splash of water as he showered, the anticipation of him coming to me almost too much to bear.

It wasn't long before he did, slipping into the bed and lying on his back with his hands behind his head. I shuffled over, nestling into him, his damp armpit hair tickling the side of my neck. He stared at the ceiling. Through the open doorway, light from the hallway spilled in, casting me in shadow but bathing Liuz in a lemon glow. He looked adorable, the muscles of his torso plainly evident, the dark stubble on his face something I wanted to lick. My pussy spasmed as I thought of that short, sharp hair brushing the insides of my thighs, between my pussy lips, and I pressed my legs together.

I smiled, content, for once, not to have sex with him. His heart thudded dully beneath my ear, and he pulled one hand out from behind his head and cradled me to him.

'We are terrible people, *Aniolku*, lying to the police, but we did what we had to do.'

Oh, Lord, he was having an attack of conscience, was feeling this harder than he'd let on.

'I know,' I said, draping my arm over his stomach and holding him tightly.

'I keep telling myself it will get better; time will make this all go away.' He paused, then, 'But there is still the issue of me owing Grant the money. His men will want it.'

'They might do, but you paid him back.'

'I do not think two fucks with you covered the cost.'

'No,' I said, leaning up on one elbow. 'You paid him back and the killers stole it.' I wasn't even shocked at my devious mind. I realised when backed into a corner, you fought however you could to keep yourself safe. 'It isn't your fault they stole the cash. I told the police they stole your money, too.'

He raised his eyebrows. 'You did?'

'Well, yes. I didn't think you'd mind.'

'No, of course I do not mind.'

'I'll tell my editor the same thing as well. So Grant's men will know it's a waste of time chasing you for money you've already paid back.'

Liuz took his other hand from beneath his head and cupped my neck. 'Ah, Hannah, you are a girl after my own heart.'

'I know.' I decided to risk pushing it. 'That's why you'll never say the stop word.'

He smiled. Sighed. 'Never say never, *Aniolku*. We do not know what the future will bring.'

I smiled back, hoping my upset didn't show, hoping

I looked blasé and in control. I realised I could never show this man how much he meant to me – not the real, deep-seated emotions that raged through me even when we were apart. It would be dangerous, like the adage goes, to put all my eggs in one basket.

'We don't,' I said brightly, settling beside him again, knowing that despite how bone-achingly tired I was, sleep would take a long while to come.

But we are together right now, tonight.

Chapter Fifteen

I slept fitfully, my dreams disjointed and macabre for the first few hours, then after I'd got up to use the toilet and returned to bed, they became vivid, bright and floaty, like sleeping amongst rainbows; smiling faces, butterflies and humming birds. The fitfulness died away and a sensation of peace and contentment soaked through my bones. It was weird, as though my worrisome brain was balancing out evil with fluffy prettiness.

So when I awoke again to the sound of the rubbish truck outside, creaking and grinding the wheelie bins to their upended positions, I felt a little stronger, and definitely better. In fact, I felt able to be the pillar for both of us; my mind was clear and my body sturdy. It was simple, as long as were together, here, safe in my flat away from Grant's men, and sticking to our story, everything would be well. We just had to lay low, be resilient and we would be fine.

I shifted on the pillow and looked at Liuz. From what

I could tell he'd slept soundly, barely moving all night. He was still on his back, the duvet settled just beneath his small, permanently erect nipples. He'd raised his left arm above his head, bent it at the elbow at a right angle. I noticed a small, almost black freckle nestled amongst his wisps of feathery armpit hair. His head was turned towards me, his stubble denser than I'd ever seen it. His mouth was slightly parted, his long lashes resting on his smooth cheeks. I took the opportunity to really study his face and, uninhibited, I scrutinised every detail. I would like to paint him in this relaxed state. Capture the slight bump in his nose, the identical creases beneath each lower eyelid, where the skin was a little more chocolaty-coloured. The Cupid's bow on his top lip that appeared deeper now, more kissable, almost angelic in its plumpness.

I loved him so much it hurt. Actually physically hurt. I'd often dreamed of falling in love, of finding 'The One'. Girls, women talked about it as though it was a wonderful thing, but for me it was agony. No one had ever taken the time to warn me of the torture and brutality of loving someone with all your heart. Of how the moment you loved someone you became vulnerable, a target for destruction. For what happened when they left you, even if just for one day? I imagined myself in the corner of the room, naked, weeping, never moving again, unable to function, unable to breathe. If Liuz left me I would surely die.

I had to keep him here.

Glancing around my room, I spotted my collection of scarves hanging on the back of the door. I slipped from the covers and stood, the cool morning air enveloping my body like an itchy blanket, and walked silently over and grabbed two identical shocking pink scarves. The material was chilled and I fisted it, one end in each hand, and gave a tug. Nice and strong. Good, my man had fine muscles.

With feline stealth, I climbed back onto the bed, grateful for my slight weight and the quiet snores that told me Liuz was in a deep sleep. Carefully, gently, I wound one scarf around the wrist tossed over his head. Then, holding my breath, secured a knot to the wooden slats on my headboard. His wrist slid upwards easily; his deep breaths didn't change.

Good, that was one arm secure.

The other one was trickier – it was on top of the duvet, resting across his abdomen, the olive tones of his flesh shocking against the creamy broderie anglaise. I slid off the bed again, tiptoed around the end and then, with lightness in my fingertips, slowly, so slowly, raised that arm above his head too.

He didn't stir. Just let me lift it up there. I stopped, once when his breaths paused, but then they resumed, deeper, and steadier than ever.

When the task was complete, I looked down at my

captive. My Liuz. Bound to my bed, sleeping like a baby. I would take care of him, make him happy, give him everything he wanted.

I had a sudden urge to kiss him awake, press my now cool skin to his hot flesh. We hadn't had sex last night, but perhaps a morning session would suit us both. Start the day off on the right foot. A new beginning for us now there was no more Beefcake, and no more worrying about emails arriving and games with words. Now we were together we should celebrate with a fuck.

But I didn't kiss him awake or suck his cock to life and ride it. Instead, I went for another shower. Enjoyed the hot water soaking into my skin and hair, and the scent of vanilla and raspberry swirling around me. It would do Liuz good to sleep after yesterday's ordeal, and I congratulated myself on harnessing my urges. At least I could linger in the shower now I knew he couldn't go anywhere.

When I went back into the bedroom, a towel secured over my breasts and my hair turbaned into another, he was awake. His eyes were lazy, upper lids heavy, and one side of his mouth curled upwards.

'Morning,' I said, bracing for a complaint about his bound arms.

'Morning, how did you sleep?'

'Not bad, considering.' I stepped over to the dressing table, reached for my body cream – cocoa butter – and squeezed a blob onto my palm. 'And you?'

'I got up about six and made tea.'

'You did?' I was surprised. I really hadn't heard a thing. I was sure he'd slept soundly next to me all night. 'I didn't hear you.' I rubbed the cream over my arms, paying extra attention to my elbows.

'No, you were asleep.'

We stared at one another for a moment, as if silently acknowledging the momentous occasion of having spent our first night together, like a real couple, but of course, that's how we were now. Fate had bound us together for all of time. History could not be rewritten even if it could be falsely documented.

'So,' he said. 'You got another little fantasy you want to tell me about?' He waggled his fingers and flexed his shoulders; the headboard rattled against the wall. 'You never mentioned you wanted to be the dominant one.' He settled his gaze on me and licked his lips. Amusement sparked within the depths of his eyes, as though I'd surprised him.

I swallowed tightly, minty toothpaste flavour spreading down my throat. Mmm, much as I'd tied him up to keep him here, perhaps we could have a little fun with me in charge for a change.

'I thought maybe I could repay you some of the pleasure you've given me, Liuz,' I suggested, making the most of the situation.

'What, sort of like when you are in my home you are

my slut, and when I am in yours I am your man-whore.'
A muscle flexed in the side of his cheek and his biceps
balled as he pulled his arms down, making the scarves
taut. 'It is a new one on me, but you have never failed
to surprise me.'

'And here was me thinking I was predictable.'

He gave a grunting noise. 'Predictable has never
appealed to me, and you, Hannah, are anything but
predictable.'

So I appealed to him. Good.

'What do you mean I'm not predictable?' I dropped
the towel to the floor and proceeded to rub more cocoa
butter cream onto my chest and belly, making sure I
was very thorough and careful not to miss even a square
millimetre of flesh.

He bit on his bottom lip and shifted beneath the duvet,
his gaze glued to my labouring hands working my naked
skin. 'Each time,' he said, 'I thought I had pushed you
too far, asked too much, you just kept on giving. When
I was sure you would say no, tell me to fuck off, you
carried on pursuing your slutty fantasies like a woman
possessed, as though you were fanatical about experi-
encing every sexual deviance you could with me.'

'Sexual deviance.' I played with the two words in my
mouth – they had a musicality to them that belied the
foulness of what they represented.

He twitched his hips. The duvet slipped down to his

belly and rested on the luscious line of tapering hair that led to his cock – a cock, I now noticed, that was rising to attention, poling the duvet with its impressive length.

'So you fancy being my man-whore then?' I asked, slipping a finger between my sex lips and giving my clit a little rub. I could already feel moisture building in my pussy. The thought of Liuz's cock in me was like flicking a switch in my sympathetic nervous system. I had no control over my body's response, it just happened.

'I should not fucking feel like doing anything with all the shit that is going down at the moment, but Jesus, Hannah, you get me so damn hard I feel like my dick might burst.'

'Oh, so are you sure you want to play?' I asked, grabbing the cocoa butter and walking over to the bed. 'You might not like being on the receiving end.'

He drew his mouth to a tight line and stared at me, unblinking.

I raised my brows.

'Fuck yes. I can handle it.'

Gripping the duvet, I flicked it to the end of the bed, exposing his body to the stark morning light with one swift movement.

He sucked in a breath, making a wet hissing sound that seemed extra loud in the quiet.

I kneeled on the bed next to him, my attention fixed on the large, blood-filled shaft in front of me. The head was swollen to a deep purple and the slit already held a bead of clear moisture.

A shiver of excitement snaked up my spine. Where to start? I wanted to give Liuz such great pleasure, but equally I didn't want to give it to him easily. Pleasure had to be earned when you were a slut or a whore or a possession of someone else's.

Feeling like I was moving in a trance, in slow motion, I flooded my palm with the cool cocoa butter then wrapped my hand around his shaft.

'Ah, fuck, that is cold,' Liuz shouted. He bucked his hips, and his upper torso jerked against his restraints. His belly contracted and his knees bent.

'Shh,' I soothed, setting up a rubbing motion that quickly began to warm the cream to body temperature. 'Just relax, let me make you feel good.'

His squeezed his eyes shut and turned his face into his upper arm, his nose denting the skin and a lock of hair falling over his eye.

I increased the pressure and with slow, deft strokes made sure no part of his cock, or balls, or the crease of his crack was uncovered, un-adored. The cream became opaque, and the dense colour of his shaft shone as my hands moved up and down, around, slipping into the deep ridge below his glans and over and through his slit.

'Oh, fuck, Hannah. I have never been one for stamina

in the morning, and you are about to fucking finish me off.'

His cheeks had risen in colour to a strawberry red, his bottom lip milky white where his top teeth were biting into it. He looked beautiful in his agonising battle with pleasure, and I knew I would paint him like this as soon as I got the chance. He would look magnificent on my wall in this frantic state.

I upped the speed, both hands assiduous in their task. My arms ached, but I didn't care – this was not about me, this was about Liuz.

His groans got louder, more abandoned.

My heart thumped and sweat pricked between my cleavage.

He was getting close, so close now.

My body was buzzing too.

'Ah, oh, God, Hannah,' he gasped, peeling back his lips to reveal his teeth in a strained grimace.

His cock became dense, more solid, and his balls packed up into his pelvis. I stared at his cock-head jigging with the rapid movements of my hands. The whole glans was swollen like a ripe plum, and the slit deep and pliant within my movements.

Another drip of pre-cum, white against the redness, leaked out. He bowed his back off the bed, his head pressed into the pillow, and lurched his hips upwards for more of my touch.

'Ah, yes, I am coming, Hannah – yes, yes – *tak, tak*.'

I released him, held my hands up high, fingers spread, and stared down at his abandoned cock.

'Oh, Jesus, oh, God, no, no, fuck it, argh!' He wailed as though in agony, his body writhing, twisting this way and that. The headboard was bouncing wildly off the wall with the full force of his furious tugging. 'What the hell are you doing?' he shouted, his cock, shiny and engorged, bobbing uncontrollably in the air.

Power seeped through me like slow-running lava, heating a trail of controlling emotions, new emotions. Watching Liuz squirming and needy, desperate for me, showed me a new, darker side to myself that I hadn't known existed.

And just when I thought I could surprise myself no more.

'Fuck, you think that is funny, do you?' Liuz snarled. 'Jesus, if only you knew.'

'Ah, baby,' I said, edging backwards when he wriggled nearer to me. 'You really wanted to come then, didn't you?'

'You know I fucking did. Christ, you cannot do that to a guy, Hannah.'

'I can, and I did.'

He was breathing fast through gritted teeth, a speck of saliva in the corner of his mouth.

'Shh,' I said quietly and tipped forward to kiss him. 'It will be worth the wait, I promise.'

212

His eyes flashed with fury and were dark with desire. For a moment he looked as though he was going to snap his head away. But he didn't, he let me kiss him, slowly and seductively, while his breathing settled.

Suddenly he yanked his arms again, with gusto, jerking both of us.

'Liuz,' I said, glancing at the delicate scarves. 'You're being a bad boy. I am going to have to tie you tighter.'

'Jesus, Hannah,' he said, crumpling up his nose. 'Just get on and ride me, will you?'

Quickly, I left the bed, plucked two more scarves from my collection – one bottle-green and one cream with tiny love hearts – and wound them around his wrists, doubling the security and tension.

'Do you want me to bind your legs as well?' I asked sternly.

He glared at me, like he would have grabbed me, shoved me down and fucked me hard and fast if he could have.

But, of course, he couldn't.

Scooting down the bed, I eased between his legs, licked my lips and watched his cock bob towards me. The engorged veins pulsated in time with my racing heartbeat.

'I never teased you like this,' he said in a shaky voice.

'I think you'll find you did, but in other ways,' I said, purposely letting my breath breeze over his moist cock, knowing the cooling effect would be stimulation in itself.

His cock strained towards my mouth, and he groaned, a deep rumbling sound that originated low in his chest.

I poked out my tongue, and carefully, cunningly, swept up the clear bead from the slit. Liuz froze. It was as if every nerve and fibre in his body had honed in on that one tiny dent. I swept my tongue around the ridge, tasting the cocoa butter and Liuz's unique, delicious, amazing dick flavour.

He was a mass of tremulous desire lying beneath me, but I wasn't faring much better. His command to ride him had been hard to disobey and I knew now, I wouldn't be far off doing just that. But I wanted him deep in my mouth first, I wanted to feel him nudge the back of my throat, feel a streak of thick pre-cum coat the base of my tongue. Parting my lips, I sank down, taking his cock as far into my mouth as I could.

'Oh, fuck,' Liuz groaned. 'Yes, that is it.'

But I only gave him one – one deep-throated ride then pulled up, releasing his cock once more so it stood upright like a startled soldier, standing to attention.

This time he didn't even bother to curse in complaint, he just moaned long and low then gabbled something in Polish.

But I was still touching him, fondling his balls and caressing the thin strip of skin towards his anus. He was so hot, so tight, so delectably lubricated, my fingers slipped and slid all over him, no part out of bounds, even the tight circle of his back passage.

Triumph welled within me, mixing with my lust to form an intoxicating rush of impatience.

He was mine and finally it was time.

With well-practised skill, I gave my clit several fast rotations, to make sure I was as turned on as Liuz. He didn't stand a chance of lasting long and I wanted us to come together. We were in perfect sync anyway, but it didn't hurt to nudge things in the right direction.

'Put your legs together,' I instructed, travelling up the bed in the same slinky, confident way a predator does when prey is cornered.

Groaning, as if moving was painful, he drew his legs together and opened his eyes. Watched me as I hovered over him, my knees bent on either side of his hips.

'You like fucking my pussy, don't you, Liuz?' I asked, spreading apart my labia with my fingertips.

'Yes, yes, oh, yes.'

'Why?'

'Oh, God, really?'

'Yes, why?' My voice was sterner and I held myself just out of reach of his thrashing hips, but kept my pelvis tilted so he could see what he was missing out on. 'Tell me.'

'Because, because you're tight, and hot, and you come so wildly, squeezing my dick until it feels like I am in Heaven.'

'Good answer,' I said, sinking a little and taking the first inch of his cock inside me.

'Ah, yes, that is it, more.'

He'd balled his fists so tight his fingers and knuckles turned white. I feared for the survival of his teeth, his jaw was tensed so hard.

I gave another inch, adoring the stretching sensations splintering through my pussy. 'Oh, Liuz, I love your dick, it's so fucking hard,' I gasped. 'So fucking hard and thick and long. Oh, it's so long.'

'Yes, baby, I am so long, and I am so fucking hard for you, take me, take all of me, fuck me, *Aniolku*, fuck me so hard, like never before, it is just us, only us.'

His words were enough to tip me over the edge. I was no longer in control of my body. I released it, gave it permission to gorge on Liuz, and snarling through the discomfort, I took him all in, as deep as he could ever go. It was as though he had become part of me, part of my core, part of my soul.

I wailed in delight; he swore loudly. A thick bulging vein on his shaft pounded against the ridge that held my G-spot.

'Yes, oh, yes, say that again, Liuz,' I cried.

'Only us, only us,' he shouted, his voice crazed, manic.

I was wild. My hips had taken on a life of their own, their main aim to satisfy my greedy clit, pumping, grinding, building up the pressure to dizzying heights.

But I wanted more, on my G-spot. I leaned back, rammed my hands on the tops of his thighs and used his legs as a brace to thrust against.

'Oh, yes, yes, fuck like that, oh, shit, I am coming,' he cried.

For a moment I thought the headboard was going to rip off the bed – it shook and rattled and creaked ominously. Liuz was heaving and bouncing beneath me, his cock barging into me, over and over as I gyrated above him, on him.

'Oh, yes, me too,' I shouted, tipping my head to the ceiling and staring at my rose-patterned lampshade. 'Yes, yes.'

Pleasure ripped through me. There was nothing gentle about this orgasm. It was frantic, hungry, uncaring of the fact it snatched my breath and made my heart skip and skip and skip.

I pulsed through the crashing waves, revelling in the feeling of Liuz pulsing through his climax. Dropped my head and watched his face contort, his lips stretching back and his eyes squeezing shut until they became horizontal black lines. Every muscle in his arms was taut, taut and straining, fighting his bonds.

I carried on riding, seeking a new, fresh climax.

'Oh, Jesus, Hannah.'

Sweat beaded in his stubble. His chest was rising and falling. But I was not ready to stop – another delicious orgasm beckoned, just seconds away.

'I cannot,' he gasped, thrashing his head on the pillow. 'Oh fuck.'

He was spent, exhausted, but his cock was still hard enough for me to bounce on and my clit was getting ready to fly again.

I dropped forward and mashed my breasts against his chest. 'Liuz, oh, fuck, yes, again, I'm coming again.'

He grunted and his breaths were noisy, storm-like, against my cheek.

My second orgasm ravaged me. I stared down into his eyes, letting him see me. The real me. Hannah. The woman who loved him.

Gradually the spasms died down in my pussy, my breathing came under control, if not back to normal, and my heart stopped throwing out odd, extra beats that thumped my ribcage.

'*Aniolku,*' he whispered. His pupils were wide and black. 'I do believe you are as bad as me.'

I giggled breathlessly, cupped his cheeks and kissed him. 'Yes, we are the same, Liuz,' I said into his mouth. 'A perfect match.'

He swept his tongue over his bottom lip, as though stealing every trace of me. 'Well, I am afraid one half of this perfect match has things to see to.' He shifted beneath me. 'So you had best untie me, so I can get some coffee and then sort out this fucked-up situation.'

Placing my hands on his chest, I straightened. His

cock was soft inside me now; I could only just feel it. 'But, Liuz, I thought you would stay here today, in my flat, with me.'

'I wish I could, but there are people I need to see. This situation affects more than just us, Hannah.'

My mind fudged. More than just us. Who else was there? There was only us. He had just said that.

Reluctantly I let my pussy release him, and I shifted sideways then stood. Stared down at a replete, sated Liuz, who was now frowning at the knots holding his arms tight.

'Hannah,' he said. 'Come on. Undo this shit.'

I had to be cruel to be kind.

I rubbed my hands together, knotting my fingers and then sliding my palms against one another. A dribble of fluid trickled down to my thigh, warm and slimy.

'Hannah!'

I swallowed tightly, let the words hover on my tongue for a moment, then said, 'I'm sorry, Liuz, but no. I am not going to untie you.'

Chapter Sixteen

I left the room and walked down the hallway, Liuz's shouts of protest muffled behind the closed door. My heart beat triple time, and I wondered what on earth had possessed me. I'd teetered on the verge of letting him go, really I had, but the thought of him walking out of my flat and not returning – even though he'd said he had nowhere else to stay – wasn't something I could handle right now. Not when I'd had a taste of what things could be like if he was here as a permanent fixture.

So I pretended he wasn't calling me, wasn't getting angrier by the second, and went to gaze at the paintings on the wall in my office-cum-studio. The scarves would hold him in place until I returned, I was sure, and, confident I could work in peace once he stopped shouting, I squirted paint onto my palette and selected a brush.

It wasn't difficult to get into that dream state I entered when doing my art. The imaginative side of me took over, sending me into a time warp where nothing existed except what I was creating – dips and swirls, hard or fuzzy lines over impressive swoops. I imagined Liuz tied up on the bed, his face contorted in the agony of pleasure, not the irritation and possible anger he was feeling now, and transferred what was in my head onto the wall.

It came out exactly as I'd seen it in my mind's eye, exactly as he'd appeared on the bed. The image made a fitting companion for the other art beside it, and I'd left enough room for another picture or two to join the mural of my time spent with him. I loved that it told a story, one only I or Liuz would understand. If anyone else were to see the painting, the series of images would come across as strange, what with the murder scene dominating the area and grabbing the attention first. Still, it was my finest art yet, more so because of the emotional attachment, and it was a shame I hadn't applied it to canvas instead. This kind of art could have sold for quite a price if displayed in the right gallery.

Would I want what equated to my private time for sale, though? Could I bear to part with it knowing other female eyes stared at Liuz in ways I wouldn't want him stared at? There was no doubt about it; he could make a woman aroused just by looking at him. Could I stand them lusting after him with the same intensity as me?

I stepped back and regarded the finished picture, took in the deep threads beside his closed eyes – eyes bunched shut in ecstasy – the contortion of his mouth, a skewed line twisted up at one corner, his hard cock jutting out, a pearl of pre-cum sitting in his slit. Yes, I think I could handle women lusting after him because, hey, he was all mine. They'd never get the chance to touch him, to make his mouth open and beg them to suck that pre-cum off his cock, to have his hands all over them, seeking out the special places that made their bodies sing.

No. He was mine.

Feeling hot and sticky, I placed my palette down and popped the brush in a glass of cleaning solution. I needed another shower – painting was such hard work – and after that I'd check on Liuz, explain why I'd left him there like that.

In the bathroom, I luxuriated beneath the warm spray, enjoying the peace and quiet. Liuz had gone silent – perhaps he'd fallen back to sleep – or maybe he lay there brooding. The image of that bloomed in my mind, and I drowned in the murky depths of those dark eyes encased in narrowed lids, anger emanating from them, a danger signal that if anyone got too close he'd bite. I was confident I had the ability to soothe his ruffled feathers. After all, he'd said he trusted me, and you couldn't get a better admission from a man than that. It made me feel safe, as though I'd surpassed that level in a relationship where uncertainty ruled and security took its place.

I stepped out of the shower and dried off, leaving the bathroom to enter the bedroom and apply cocoa butter cream again. At the bedroom door, though, I paused, suddenly unsure of the reaction awaiting me behind it. I took a deep breath and went inside, relief bleeding into me that Liuz greeted me with a broad smile.

'Very funny, *Aniolku*,' he said, finishing off with a chuckle. 'I get what you were doing. Exerting some control of your own. I understand that.'

He smiled again, wider this time, and I smiled back.

'Although I love your dominant side,' I said, stepping over to the bed, 'I wanted you to see I like being dominant myself, show you how much I have to offer, how sex can be when we're both crazy with control.' I untied one pair of scarves with a bit of difficulty – him wrenching them had tightened the knots – and hoped he'd got the message that I wasn't ready for him to leave just yet. 'Can you imagine that? How great it'll be?'

'Fuck, yeah. I can imagine it.' He circled his freed hand, wrist an angry shade of red, much like the colour I'd used when painting the blood for the murder scene.

I leaned over to untie the second scarf but the position pulled on the muscles at my waist. Climbing onto him, seating my slit directly onto his cock – God, I could just ride him again now – I reached out and dug my thumbnail between two stubborn, tight arcs of fabric. They wouldn't give, so I undid the knot with my teeth, conscious of my breast brushing his shoulder. I tossed the scarf on the bed and sat back, looking down at him, waiting for a signal as to what would happen next. Would he fuck me again or get up with the intention of going out and seeing to things?

'Come on,' he said. 'We need to eat. I need coffee.'

He patted my thigh, and I shifted over, sitting cross-legged on the bed while he got up. I loved watching him dress and marvelled at the fact this was the first morning of many to come where I could indulge in seeing how he zipped up his jeans, the waistband fitting snuggly about his hips. How he tugged a T-shirt over his head and settled the hem about his waist. How those gorgeous muscles of his screamed out how toned they were even from beneath fabric.

He sat on the bed to put on his shoes and socks, glancing around once to throw a wink over his shoulder. We were OK, everything was going to be all right. I knew it would be.

'So,' he said, walking to the door. 'What do you have in to eat? Bacon? Eggs?'

I thought about what was in the fridge. 'Neither. Cereal or milk is about the limit for breakfast today.'

'Ah, and I wanted our first breakfast together to be the full English. I noticed a little shop down the road when I came here last night. Do you want me to go out and buy what we need?'

'No,' I said, a little too quickly. 'I'll go. You get that coffee you need.'

Before he could protest, I leaped off the bed and yanked my clothes on, my jeans tight and constricting from their recent wash. Liuz left the room, and I heard the kitchen tap gush water. With a T-shirt and sweater on, I slid my feet into a pair of training shoes and whipped a brush through my hair, excitement at doing my first 'shop' for our first meal together sending me giddy. I dashed down the hallway, making another mental note to get a lock for my office door, and poked my head into the kitchen.

Liuz had put the kettle on, the rumble of it starting to boil a pleasant sound, and leaned with his ass against the sink unit, arms folded across his chest. I looked at him to judge whether he was relaxed or just pretending, but he glanced over at me with that broad smile again and I knew he was going to stay.

'I'll just be off then. Won't be a minute,' I said. 'Do you want the full works? Fried bread and everything?'

'Please,' he said, taking two cups off the mug tree and scraping the coffee canister across the worktop towards him.

He opened drawers in search of a spoon, I guessed, and a swell of happiness surged inside me. Liuz appeared so at home in my little kitchen. So right.

'OK. I'll, um, I'll get going.'

He raised one hand while rooting in the drawer with another, and I turned away, that image firmly imprinting itself in my mind. I grabbed my bag from the living room and left the flat, almost running down the street towards the shop. He was going to stay, I knew that, but still, rushing a little wouldn't hurt, would it?

In the shop, I grimaced at the amount of customers milling about. Since when had this place ever been so busy? A queue snaked down the centre aisle, people clutching pints of milk and folded-over newspapers to their chests, some with heavy baskets by their sides. I picked up a basket of my own and headed to the chiller, pleased to find plenty of bacon packets on the shelf. Did he prefer his smoked? I wasn't sure so put one of each in my basket, feeling like a proper woman with a man at home waiting for me to return with the shopping. I selected a loaf of bread, some baked beans and a small bottle of cooking oil, a local newspaper – just in case there was something in it we needed to see – and another jar of coffee. If I remembered rightly, there wasn't enough to last the day if both of us were drinking it. Come to think of it, I'd better get milk too.

I tacked myself on to the end of the queue, which had grown longer as I'd shopped, and bit back a mutter of annoyance. I missed Liuz already, imagined he'd be on his second cup of coffee by now, perhaps wondering where I was, why it was taking me so long. I went through my return to the flat in my head, me waffling about the damn queue, and wouldn't you just know someone had a trolley full of goods ahead of me? Why hadn't they gone to the main supermarket? Why was there only one person manning the tills? A typical Post Office scenario, but I wouldn't storm off in a huff, leaving my basket on the floor. No, we were going to have our full English breakfast this morning, sitting side-by-side on my sofa – our sofa – knees touching.

There was a commotion up ahead. Something to do with an item not scanning and the shop assistant needing a co-worker to fetch him another of the same item. Why wasn't the co-worker behind a till too? I tapped my foot, getting a little impatient now, and lowered the basket to the floor. To pass the time, I reached down for the newspaper, scouring the front page expecting to see a big splash about the murders. There wasn't one. The main tale was about a resident irate about the state of the paving slabs outside her house. She'd fallen and broken her ankle, and wasn't that what we paid taxes for, to have streets that weren't potential death threats? In the top right-hand corner, two inches by three, was a snippet about two men being gunned down in a private residence. No names, no gory details, just that police were treating it as suspicious.

I breathed out, tension leaking away. I hadn't even been aware of my muscles being inhabited by the rigidity of stress until it was gone. The line shifted forward, the till scanner thankfully bleeping away again. I folded the newspaper and dropped it into the basket, knowing Liuz would be pleased the events in his flat didn't warrant anything but a tiny mention.

At last, my turn came, and I resisted making a caustic remark about the state of the service in here. Instead, I dumped my basket on the counter and watched the worker bag my things, then paid and left the shop as though the devil chased me. I didn't like being apart from Liuz, clearly, and although I knew I'd become attached, I hadn't realised just how attached until now. I needed to see him, to know he was there, to have his presence even if he didn't feel like talking. And we didn't need to talk, did we? No, we could say what we wanted just by looking at one another – or we would do once we'd been together for a while longer.

I turned my key in the lock, pushing the door with my hip – it had taken to sticking lately – and blustered into my flat. The sound of the TV filtered from the living room, a news channel if the monotone of a bored male was anything to go by, and I smiled at the thought of Liuz sprawled on my sofa, waiting for news of what had happened to reach the London masses. Waiting for me to get back.

I went into the kitchen, dumping the bags on the counter, and wandered into the living room with a casual air about me, as though I came home to having a man in my place all the time.

He wasn't there.

I frowned and walked down the hall, checking my bedroom. Finding it empty, I stood outside the closed bathroom door and listened for sounds from within. There weren't any, but instead of lurking about when he was having a moment to himself, I returned to the kitchen and unloaded the bags. Job done, I flicked the kettle on, noting the second cup he'd taken from the mug tree still stood on the counter with coffee and sugar in the bottom, a spoon leaning against the side. His cup was in the sink, so I grabbed another and made us both a hot drink.

With the cups full and steaming, I called out, 'Coffee's ready! Just going to start breakfast! Chop chop!'

I smiled, bubbling over with the new sensation of domesticity for two, popped a few sausages on a baking tray and slid them into the oven. Bacon rashers laid out on the grill pan, baked beans in a small saucepan on the hob, I selected a knife from the drawer in order to slice onions and mushrooms. Unsure if he even liked them, I put the knife down and went back to the bathroom so I could check. I knocked on the door.

'Liuz? You OK in there?'

No response.

My heart picked up speed, and my thoughts immediately went to my office. If he was in there, I'd – No, he'd said he wouldn't look, wouldn't invade my private space, and I believed him. I knocked on the bathroom door again and, when silence greeted me, turned the handle and pushed the door open.

The bathroom was empty.

Spare room. He'd be in the spare room.

He wasn't.

That only left my office, and I took a moment while standing in the hallway to think about how I was going to handle this. Was it so bad that he'd gone inside, wanting to know the other part of me? It was sweet, really, him wanting to see my work, to find out what made me tick. But what if he didn't like what he saw? What if my subject matter shocked him? Oh, my art wasn't ugly – different maybe, but not ugly – so I wasn't worried about his reaction to it in that way, but him being the main focus might be a bit of a shock.

Or would it? Maybe he'd take it that I cared about him so much that I had to express it in the only way I knew how, by committing his image to the wall in paint, something tangible and not just an emotion. How would I feel if it was the other way around? I'd get that warm and fuzzy feeling that I was so adored my man thought of nothing but me, that I dominated his thoughts and he needed to paint me, wanted to paint me.

I went inside.

Liuz wasn't there either.

Panic started as a tingle of nerves in the pit of my stomach then broadened out to a nasty set of pinches that combined into a painful knot of apprehension, growing up my windpipe and settling in my chest. I had the urge to run, to scour my flat and check the cupboards, the wardrobe in my room in case he was playing a trick on me, testing to see how much I cared. But I didn't. I stayed rooted to the spot, telling myself he'd just gone out to sort a few things, that he'd be back once he'd smoothed over whatever the hell needed smoothing over, and we'd carry on with our lives as I'd planned, happy and content with each other.

Yes, that was what had happened. He'd just nipped out. That was all.

God, I was so paranoid. I needed to get a grip.

I lifted one hand to my chest, as though the warmth of my palm would settle the pounding throb there, the *tick-tick-tick* of the raging pulse in my neck. Taking a deep, settling breath, I stared at the mural as though looking at it through Liuz's eyes, trying to imagine what he would see, how he would see it.

They were beautiful, I could admit that – they really were my finest work. I scanned across from the first to the last, sucking in a breath at how Liuz affected me, how even a painted image of him stirred desire within me and a longing to get to know him, every last thing. My chest hurt with the weight of my emotions, feelings surging through me at speed, and I staggered to the side and leaned my shoulder against the doorjamb.

And frowned.

Something wasn't right. Something was off.

I cocked my head, trying to work it out. The pictures were exactly the same, the hues the ones I'd chosen, the brush strokes unchanged. So what was the matter? I narrowed my eyes, searching every inch of those pictures for the clue to what was bugging me.

There it was, what looked like a very faint smudge of black, a whisper of a brush tip, the paint barely there to the untrained eye. I moved closer to the wall, narrowing my eyes some more, cocking my head further, stomach bunching as that smudge became what it was, turned from an innocent wisp into so much more.

I stared at it for a long time, uncomprehending, then leaned closer just to make sure my eyes weren't deceiving me. On the last painting, the one of my darling Liuz bound by pink scarves, was something I had never wanted to see. It was on his foot, at an angle, the use of a black biro on my artwork obscene and totally out of place. Totally wrong.

One word, that's all it took to shatter my world.

Kilimanjaro.

Chapter Seventeen

One year later

Heartbreak, I discovered, was like the devil jabbing at every inch of my body with his cruel, merciless fork, over and over and over. Twisting my intestines so eating was impossible. Snatching my breath so sharply it was hard to breathe, and when I lay in bed at night, sobbing until my face puffed up like a balloon, I would have preferred someone to peel out my spine, nape to tailbone, and whip me with it than have to wake up, again, to the knowledge that Liuz had left me.

That Liuz had written the stop word.

How could he? How could he be so blinkered, so blind to what we had? We were great together. It was us against the world. The underworld.

So it was just as well I had a plan to get destiny back on track. Kilimanjaro had its uses for a while, but that time had been and gone. There was so much more to think about now, and its significance in my life was about as important as a distant planet on the outer edge of the solar system.

Three weeks after Liuz had left me, he was allowed back into his home. I didn't know where he'd stayed in the interim, but when he moved in again, the window had been repaired and a new carpet had been delivered and fitted two days previously.

To start with, I wondered how he could go back there. To the murder scene. But spying on him, from behind my faithful tree, and watching him open the curtains and stare wistfully out at the blue sky I suddenly understood. There weren't just gruesome memories in that place. There were also memories of lust and love, wild abandon and giving in to insatiable desires. I understood him, really I did. For in that bedsit was where we first discovered the pleasure of one another. Liuz and Hannah. It was where our lives together had properly begun.

I desperately wanted to go to him. Hold him. Remind him what it was he loved about me. But I couldn't. There were things to be seen to first. I had to prioritise and Liuz's safety was top of that list. Especially now he was back there.

Using the pen name Aniolku Meadows, I wrote a first-person report about the murders, being sure to add in that all payments had been settled by Biros so Beefcake's men wouldn't hassle him. When I subbed it to my ed, he was beyond pleased with its gruesome details and it went to print the very next day along with a picture of 78 Woodstone Road with a boarded-up windowpane.

But keeping Liuz safe was a two-step plan for there were others out there who were also a threat. People, women, who might try and take my place, and now, especially now, with this new and exciting development in my life, that risk had to be eliminated.

Officer Lederman was cool and calm when I called and asked for an appointment. In fact, he came to me. I didn't even have to go to the police station.

But before he visited I added a bolt onto the door of my Liuz room. My paintings were for my eyes only. Liuz's reaction had proven that the rest of the world was not ready for my work. My erotic and macabre blend of art was obviously an acquired taste, and I wished I could have introduced it to him slowly. Explained the details and the reasons for each picture. Made him see beyond the images to the emotions, the story, the way the colours and strokes celebrated my undying love for him.

If only he'd stayed out of that room. If only he'd obeyed me, done as he'd been told. Life would be very different for us. He would still be here rather than sitting in a cell, and he wouldn't be missing out on these first precious months.

As I disembarked the bus and stared up at the high, grey

walls of HMP Wandsworth, a cool wind circled my face, flapping my once again long hair across my cheeks. The black door before me was large and solid, with thick iron bolts and hinges. Holding in inmates, holding in my future.

My mind was full of 'what if' thoughts and they'd spiralled during the journey and formed coiled, hard knots of anxiety. I hadn't felt like that since the day I told Officer Lederman about Liuz's involvement in counterfeit alcohol. That day I'd been nervous, on edge, but only because I couldn't be sure my plan was going to work. Liuz could have been locked away for too short a period of time, or too long. As it turned out, he would be free by Christmas, having received a lenient sentence for being a middleman as opposed to a main dealer, and also for good behaviour. Having him home for Christmas was going to be wonderful and what I prayed for every night.

Stepping into the prison, along with another visitor, also a woman, I took a pen from a guard and signed the visitor's book. The pen felt slimy in my sweaty hands, the same way it had when I'd filled in Roksana's birth certificate. This day had been a long time coming, and it took considerable effort on my part to ensure the stars were lined up for us, for all three of us. But it was going to be wonderful. How could it not be? But even with all my efforts, nerves still rattled in my stomach and weakened my knees. I rehearsed the scenario about to be realised, once again, and pictured the perfect outcome.

The corridor leading to the visitation suite smelled of dinner – vegetables and stew – and reminded me of my comprehensive school; the long stretch of hard floor, the pale-green walls, the absence of furniture or homely comforts. At the far end a heavy door led into a large room about the size of an assembly hall. I'd expected to see Liuz behind toughened glass, us having to use one of those telephones to talk to one another, our palms pressed so hard against the divider our skin turned yellow-white. But that was clearly not going to be the case. I was pleased, though. This suited my needs much better even if the scenario in my head had to be quickly rewritten.

I walked straight ahead, following a guard whose keys and baton rattled at his waist. The crackle of menace in the air told me this was no school. This was a very different place altogether. Red stacker chairs were set either side of white tables, the walls painted the same insipid shade of green as the corridors, and closed-circuit television cameras hung from the ceiling. Men in dark-blue, standard-issue clothing, hunched at tables, arms folded, scowls in place. Some had visitors, some sat alone, smoking, eyeing up me and Roksana. A woman, tattoos up her neck, slipped a package to a man beneath their table. The look she gave me, when she caught me staring, guaranteed my silence. I had no desire to come face-to-face with her on my way home. She looked as hard as any of the blokes in the room.

Liuz sat with his head low and appeared engrossed in a hangnail on his right thumb. His hair was shorter, and he wore the same dark clothing as every other prisoner.

We stopped directly in front of him. 'Hi, Liuz,' I said quietly.

His attention snapped up. He leaped to his feet, pushing his chair back, the legs scraping loudly on the floor.

'Hannah,' he gasped, widening his eyes and dropping his mouth slack. 'What the fuck?'

The guard stepped over to him, scowled and nodded to the chair.

Liuz sat back down with ritualised obedience and spread his hands on the table, fingers separated wide

I stayed standing, cradling Roksana's nappy-fat bottom through the carrier. 'How have you been?' I asked. My heart was thumping wildly. Being so near him, seeing his beautiful face after all this time, was releasing a gush of emotions inside me. Combined with excitement and adrenaline, my blood had become a heated soup of turmoil, my knees weaker than ever.

His gaze dipped to the dark-haired bundle strapped to my body, then up to my face, then back to Roksana. Rapid movements of his eyes as he balled his hands into fists on the table and tensed his shoulders towards his ears. It became clear he wasn't going to fill me in on how he had been. But that was OK, I had expected him to be pretty speechless at this point.

'There's someone you should meet,' I said, carefully extracting Roksana from the sling, pulling out her tiny limbs and supporting her head. 'This is Roksana.'

On cue, Roksana opened her dark eyes. Then she pouted her little rosebud lips, as if offering Liuz a kiss.

'Roksana,' I said, manoeuvring her so he could see her properly. 'Say hello to your daddy.'

Liuz shoved a hand through his hair, making a dark tuft stick up oddly. I itched to smooth it down. He swallowed, once, twice. Rubbed his fingers over his forehead. The cuff of his top fell up his arm slightly, revealing a scabbed wound, red and angry. I tried not to look at it. Tried not to think how he could have got it.

'Roksana?' he whispered.

'Yes, it means dawn, in Polish. New beginnings, fresh start.'

'Yes, yes. I know what it means. But ...'

'She is yours,' I said, finally taking a seat.

The hard plastic dug into the bony protrusion on my back. I had lost weight since having Roksana. Probably a bit too much. It was hard work looking after a child when you were completely alone. Feeding myself was not always a priority. I could only hope that when Liuz saw me naked again he would still enjoy the look and feel of my body.

'I, Jesus, Hannah. I had no idea, why didn't you –?' He shook his head.

I wasn't sure if he had blinked yet since setting eyes on his child.

'Tell you?'

He nodded, a stiff little movement, his gaze glued on Roksana. 'Yes, why didn't you tell me you were having a child?'

I settled Roksana in the crook of my arm and began to spin my web of lies. 'I didn't realize I was pregnant for ages, not until it was too late to, you know, do anything about it. And then, when I did find out, I realised how much I wanted her. Our child, our daughter. There was only you, Liuz, we didn't use protection that last time, do you remember? We were so carried away with our lovemaking, all we could think of was one another.'

He closed his eyes for a few long seconds, as if remembering back to that wonderful morning. Well, the start of it anyway.

When he opened his eyes again, I brushed my lips over Roksana's head, hair as soft as an angel's whisper. 'I just wished you had been there, Liuz, to see her the day she was born.'

'Well, yeah, er, me too, but kind of hard when I am banged up in here.'

I could almost hear the cogs of his mind working, his mouth barely keeping up with his thoughts.

'I went to your flat when I found out I was pregnant. But there was someone else living there. He said you were in prison, so I rang Officer Lederman. He told me that you were serving time for selling-on counterfeit alcohol.' I paused and shook my head. 'I am so sorry, Liuz. What happened? How did they find out? What with Beef – I mean, Grant – being dead.'

Liuz twisted his mouth and shrugged. 'I do not know. Some anonymous tip-off, apparently. Bastard. I'll kill them if I ever get my hands on them.'

I breathed a sigh of relief. Officer Lederman had promised me anonymity. It seemed he had lived up to his word.

'So when will you be out?'

'Eight weeks and it cannot come soon enough.' He nodded at Roksana. 'How old is she?'

'Three months.'

'Can I hold her?'

'Of course, she's your baby too, Liuz.'

He glanced at the guard who'd told him to sit earlier. Our conversation had clearly been overheard, because the guard nodded and gave a 'go ahead' wave of his palm.

Standing, I passed Ana over to her father, my heart swelling, my breath held. This an act usually performed in a hospital delivery suite, but not for us, not for Roksana – she was meeting her father in prison, in a scary big room full of mad and bad people.

Liuz held her inexpertly, his big hands awkward on

her. Carefully, I repositioned his fingers so he supported her head and her body sat within his arms. My fingertips brushed his forearm, and a familiar tingle of longing raced through me. I wanted Liuz now as much as I had right in the very beginning. Perhaps even more so.

He dipped his head to hers, shut his eyes and breathed in deep. I knew what he was doing. It was the same thing I did. He was drawing in her heavenly baby smell, powder and petals. It was addictive, that smell, and the need to inhale it repeatedly a very instinctual one that couldn't be ignored.

Roksana had seen very few adults other than me, just a few medical staff, and I had been terrified that when she saw her father she would wail. I'd made sure I'd fed her and changed her nappy just before the visit to ensure she would be on her best behaviour, but it still couldn't be guaranteed. Though it seemed I had worried needlessly, because crying wasn't going to be the case. Instead, she just looked up at Liuz, her long lashes fluttering as she struggled to focus on a new face.

'She is beautiful,' Liuz said, gazing into eyes that were mirror images of his own. 'Really, so beautiful.' He looked up, tears brimming on his lower lids. 'Oh, fuck, Hannah, what the hell are we going to do?'

'It's OK,' I said, reaching over the table and once again resting my fingers on his forearm, 'really, it's going to be fine.'

He shook his head then looked back down at Roksana. 'How can it be? Look at me. I am such a fucking loser.'

'No, no don't you ever say that.' My voice was stern. 'You are a clever, independent, determined man, and this is all going to be fine. I've thought it through.'

He sucked his lips in on themselves, as if holding in emotions he didn't want to give words to.

I allowed him a few seconds to control himself. I knew he would be like this. He acted all tough but he had a soft heart, my Liuz.

'What exactly do you mean?' he asked eventually.

'When you come out you can be a father to her, Liuz. I want you to be, so does Roksana. Every little girl needs a daddy.'

'But, Hannah, are you not mad at me? I just fucking walked out, left you, with just ... with just that word.'

A shard of pain sliced through me at the memory, but I braced against it and stuck to my plan. 'Of course I was upset, we went through a lot together. I had strong feelings for you, Liuz, you know that.'

'I just could not fucking cope,' he said, shaking his head. 'When I saw that wall, with all those crazy paintings you had done. Seeing it all there, in front of me. It made me realise that I had dragged you into something so depraved and evil.' He dropped his head. 'I felt like such a nasty bastard and I was ashamed to have ever allowed you to become involved. You are a good woman, a sweet girl, and I knew you deserved more, even if you didn't believe that you did. You could do much better than me, Hannah.'

'That's not true.' I fiddled with a buckle on the baby sling. 'There was nothing conventional about our relationship, Liuz. From the very first email to our very last fuck, we were living on the edge, the boundaries of what was acceptable to both of us.'

'Yeah, I suppose you are right.'

He dipped his head and sniffed Roksana's head again. Her little fingers flailed as if reaching for him, and he tentatively allowed her to grasp his pinky.

Tears nipped at my eyes. The sight of them together was almost overwhelming.

'Well, it's gone now, the mural. I had to make that room into a nursery. I covered it in pink and painted Disney princesses on it. She loves to lie in her cot and stare at Snow White especially.'

A small smile tugged at Liuz's mouth. 'I used to like that story when I was a child. The dwarves were funny.'

I allowed a moment of triumph. I was getting to him. 'So when you come out, in eight weeks' time, where are you going to live? Your place has been rented out to someone else.'

'I am not sure. There are a bunch of busybodies who help sort out shit like that.'

I tensed. This was my big moment. 'Why don't you come and live with us?'

He dragged his attention from Roksana and settled a brooding stare on me. 'Why would you offer me that?' His voice was incredulous.

All the other noises in the room faded. Although the air was cool it was like I was in my own hot bubble. Sweat pricked and my pulse raced. 'Because you are the father of my child, Liuz. I, we, want you there.'

His jaw tensed and a small muscle twitched. 'I do not know.' He shook his head.

A bilious wave of nausea rose like a flame up my gullet. 'It seems the perfect solution. Come and stay, for a while, at least. Get to know Roksana. She'll be sitting up soon, crawling. Don't miss these things, Liuz.'

Roksana squirmed in his arms. He made a soothing, shushing noise and rocked her gently. She quieted and stared up at him, as though as fascinated by her father as he was with her. As I was with him, too.

'See, you're a natural,' I said, wringing my hands then knotting them on the cool table, squeezing until my knuckles paled.

He said nothing, a silence extending between us. A silence I wanted to fill with words of persuasion, temptation, begs and pleas. I had to be with him. I had to have him in my life. This couldn't all be for nothing. Going through having a baby, all alone, his time in prison, he couldn't just let it be in vain.

Eventually he spoke. 'I think I just want to go home.'

'But, but you can't, I told you, the place has been let out to someone else.'

He shook his head. 'No, you misunderstood me.'

'I did?'

'Yes, home, to Poland.'

It was as though a ton of lead weights had been dropped in my stomach. My head spun. Never had I bargained on this. Him wanting to leave the country.

'But, why? I wrote the article, for the paper, the one you wanted me to, saying that all debts had been settled. There is nothing to fear if you stay.'

He cocked his head. 'I did not know you had done that, thank you. But I have contacts at home, friends, good friends. I can get a job doing something honest, hold my head up again, make something of my life.'

'But what about Roksana? You won't be able to see her grow up if you're in Poland.'

What about me? What about me? Don't leave me, not again.

I felt as though my world was about to implode. Collapse around me. I didn't think I could pick up the pieces, especially if all hope was lost.

He shifted slightly, extended a hand over the table and reached for my clasped ones. '*Aniolku,*' he said, his tone gentle, soothing, and his gaze holding mine. 'Please, come with me. We can make a life together for our daughter, for ourselves.'

I willed my body still when I wanted to spin and twirl. Had I heard right? Me and Roksana go to Poland? 'You want me to come with you?' I whispered shakily.

'Yes, both of you. It seems the only solution. You are right, Hannah, what we had was good. Weird, fucked-up weird to be precise, but hell, there was something hot going on.' His gaze dropped to my chest, and he swept the tip of his tongue over his lower lip. 'I have thought about our time together while I have been in here. It has kept me going sometimes, remembering the fantasies we played out. Of course, I try not to think of Grant inside you, that still makes me feel sick.' He pulled down the corners of his mouth. 'But what we did and your hot little body –' He leaned closer, his hand tightening on mine, and dropped his voice to a whisper. 'Your wet pussy and tight ass, I miss it. I miss you.'

A sob was ballooning in my chest. 'I've missed you too.'

He tipped his mouth into a smile. A smile I adored, a smile I would walk to the end of the world for.

A bell suddenly rang, signalling the end of visiting time. Liuz glanced at the guard to his left, who nodded at Roksana then at me, wordlessly instructing that it was time for Liuz to hand back his daughter.

I took her and she let out a mew of complaint. She'd clearly fallen in love with Liuz as much as I had. I couldn't blame her. He was perfect.

'Will you come next week?' he asked, remaining seated the same way all the other prisoners were, even though visitors were shuffling and moving around now.

'Do you want me to?'

He nodded. 'Yes, and please, promise me you will think about it, coming to Poland with me. I will try and make this right for us, I swear it.'

The decision had already been made. How could I not follow the man I loved, the father of my child? It was the easiest decision of my life. I was going to live in Poland.

I slotted Roksana into her strapping and settled her warm little body against my chest. Stood.

'*Aniolku*,' Liuz said, reaching for my hand again and bringing my knuckles to his lips.

A tiny current of electricity infused my whole body. It was a feeling I had missed so much and longed to have in my life again.

'There will be no more stop words,' he said. 'Not now we have Roksana. This, us, will go on forever.' His gaze was steely now, as if projecting his sincerity with his eyes.

'Yes,' I said. 'Forever.'

'So you will think about it. Being mine, coming to my homeland?'

I looked down into his drawn but handsome face. It was full of earnestness, full of hope.

I thought of how my life had changed since our first dirty words to one another. Then I was a journalist, an

independent woman, seeking a little fun with my fantasies. Now I was a mother, to all intents and purposes
an accessory to murder too, but I was also in love and
I wouldn't change a thing about the last year of my life.
For Liuz was my everything and I would be strong for
both of us. There was nothing to fear. I had the power
to keep us happy and together, forever.

'Yes, Liuz. I will visit next week, and although Poland
would be a big change for us, I will think about it.'

www.ingramcontent.com/pod-product-compliance
Ingram Content Group UK Ltd.
Pitfield, Milton Keynes, MK11 3LW, UK
UKHW022302180325
456436UK00003B/184